Mason

He was everything she wanted in a man and no matter how hard she'd resisted, Lianne had fallen in love with him.

She loved him. There, she'd finally said it. But now that she had made that realization, what would she do?

She knew she didn't want a relationship, because that would mean giving up the independence that had become so much a part of her life. Yes, she wanted to make love to him, but would the two short weeks they might have together be enough?

Though marriage was rarely on her mind, Lianne did want happiness, and eventually she wanted to get married. But she couldn't think of marriage now. She had too many plans.

So where did she go from here? First, she needed to be honest with Mason. She needed to tell him the truth.

Before she lost her nerve, Lianne picked up the phone and dialed Mason's room.

WAYNE JORDAN

is a high school teacher who lives on the island of Barbados. He has a B.A. in English and linguistics and an M.A. in applied linguistics from the University of the West Indies. As founder and editor-in-chief of *Romance in Color,* his passion has always been the promotion of the African-American romance. His debut release, *Capture the Sunrise,* part of the *Slow Motion* anthology written by Arabesque's first two male authors, received a Reviewer's Choice Award from the *Road to Romance* Web site and a 4-star rating from *Romantic Times BOOKclub.* *Embrace the Moonlight* is his sophomore release.

Wayne Jordan

EMBRACING
THE MOONLIGHT

KIMANI
PRESS

If you purchased this book without a cover you should be aware
that this book is stolen property. It was reported as "unsold and
destroyed" to the publisher, and neither the author nor the
publisher has received any payment for this "stripped book."

This story is dedicated to my aunt, Sandra Wilkinson.
You have been my strength, my inspiration, my friend.

Acknowledgment
To my new friends of the RWA Online Chapter.
Thanks for your support.
To the talented R. Barri Flowers A.K.A. Devon Vaughn Archer—
talent extraordinaire—your commitment to the craft
of writing is a source of inspiration and motivation.

To the ONE who gives me strength each day.
I am humbled by your unwavering love for me.

 KIMANI PRESS™

ISBN-13: 978-1-58314-781-8
ISBN-10:   1-58314-781-0

EMBRACING THE MOONLIGHT

Copyright © 2006 by Wayne Jordan

All rights reserved. The reproduction, transmission or utilization
of this work in whole or in part in any form by any electronic, mechanical
or other means, now known or hereafter invented, including xerography,
photocopying and recording, or in any information storage or retrieval
system, is forbidden without written permission. For permission please
contact Kimani Press, Editorial Office, 233 Broadway, New York, NY
10279 U.S.A.

All characters in this book have no existence outside the imagination of
the author and have no relation whatsoever to anyone bearing the same
name or names. They are not even distantly inspired by any individual
known or unknown to the author, and all incidents are pure invention.
Any resemblance to actual persons, living or dead, is entirely coincidental.

® and TM are trademarks. Trademarks indicated with ® are registered in
the United States Patent and Trademark Office, the Canadian Trade Marks
Office and/or other countries.

www.kimanipress.com

Printed in U.S.A.

Dear Reader,

I hope you enjoyed reading *Embracing the Moonlight,* the second book in my BUCHANAN BROTHERS series. Though Mason and Lianne's story was a difficult one to write, I'm pleased with the final result and hope you are, too.

Thanks to all my fans who wrote me about my debut release, *Capture the Sunrise.* I really appreciate your kind words. I'm sure you enjoyed seeing Taurean, Alana and Melissa again in *Embrace the Moonlight.*

In my next Arabesque novel, Daniel Buchanan will face personal tragedy and loss. His story will be one in which he must confront faith and love.

Be sure to visit my Web site, www.waynejordan.com, or e-mail me at author@waynejordan.com. I can also be found hosting the Kimani Press community on the Harlequin Web site at www.eHarlequin.com.

May God continue to bless you.

Until...

Wayne Jordan

Chapter 1

Mason Sinclair tried with all his willpower not to stare at the two firm breasts right before his eyes. He groaned, the discomfort a bit too much to handle as he felt the familiar stirring that took place whenever Nurse Debby came near.

He hated having no control over his reaction to her.

He didn't want to feel anything.

"So how's my favorite patient doing?" Nurse Debby's voice whispered, its huskiness slipping between the sheets to taunt his nether regions.

Mason wished she'd go away. He didn't want to feel alive. He didn't deserve to be the one living.

"I'll be back in a few minutes. I need to get clean sheets for your bed." She smiled before slipping quietly from the room.

His partner's face flashed before his eyes. Sam had been like a brother to him. They had been partners for more than ten years and there was nothing they didn't know about each other. But then, just a few months ago, it had all ended. A single bullet and Sam was gone. His own career flushed down the toilet.

Somehow, something had gone wrong. He knew it wasn't his fault. Yet, the guilt gnawed at his gut until he ached for the oblivion that came with the pain medication the doctor had prescribed.

He'd wanted to be the one to tell Sam's wife, Clair, and comfort her and the kids. Instead, Clair had been the one to do the comforting. Her husband had passed away and still she'd been at the hospital while he'd undergone surgery. She'd been the one to try to pull him out of the depression when he'd first realized he'd never be totally whole again. Yes, he'd been told he would walk again, but not with the grace and agility that was needed for his line of work.

In a sense, the news was a relief to him. He'd become disillusioned with the job for the past few years, but never expected that his way out would be a bum leg that didn't function as well as it should.

His days as an agent were over. He didn't want to be responsible for the life of another man, woman or child again. He was going to get one of those safe jobs—a teacher or maybe an accountant.

He'd never hold a gun in his hands again.

The door swung open and Nurse Debby swayed inside, her ample hips moving seductively. When she reached his bed, she smiled. Again, his body responded.

"Okay, it's time for your bath," she said gently.

He felt laughter bubbling inside. Nurse Debby was in for a *big* surprise. There was no way he could bring the situation under control before she slipped the sheet from around him.

He closed his eyes, willing himself to think of pain and sadness.

He felt the soft touch of her hand….

Ten minutes later, all fresh and clean, he waved goodbye as she left the room. She had been as always the perfect example of professionalism, but his warped imagination continued to weave a wild scenario of unbridled passion. He wiggled his toes, relieved to feel the movement. It never ceased to amaze him every time he did it. It was his reassurance that he was not dreaming. For days after he'd been shot, his leg had refused to function. Then one night, he'd awoken to excruciating pain as the muscles in his leg had clenched in spasm after spasm.

He'd cried with relief.

Now, two months later, he was making progress. He could walk with the help of a cane. He was no longer fit for the Bureau, but he didn't care. He had no intention of returning to a job that placed friends and lovers, husbands and wives in danger.

He had made that decision long before he was told he'd walk again. His job had ceased to give him any enjoyment. Sam had felt the same way. They'd both planned to leave.

For Sam, however, it was too late.

After the surgery, Mason had thanked God for giving him his life back. There was no way he was going to endanger it again now that he'd been given a second chance.

His feelings confused him. There were times he wished he had been the one to die. It wasn't as though he embraced death, but it pained him deeply to think of Sam's children having to grow up without their father.

He hated hospitals, but most of all he hated the looks of pity everyone wore when they thought he wasn't looking. Nurse Debby, however, was different. She was an interesting diversion from his ennui. She was the kind of woman whom most men found attractive. Long hair, nice ample bosom, but what stimulated him most was the fact that she'd refused to let him give up and had challenged him each time she'd entered his room.

She'd nagged and prodded, but she made him want to live again and fight to walk. Though she'd not been able to convince him to return to the Bureau, she'd pulled him out of the sulking he'd seemed too willing to embrace when he'd first been told he may never walk again.

Mason wished his father were still alive. It was moments like these when he wanted his father. *Sure,* he was forty years old, but his heart ached for the man who'd been there for him for as long as he could remember. When his father had passed away just when he'd entered the Bureau, he'd been devastated, but he knew his father would be proud of him. He had been unable to imagine life without the man who'd been there for him.

The pain had lessened over the years, but memories of the times they'd spent together were still vivid.

At least there was something to look forward to today. His mother was coming. A visit from his mother had become one of the highlights of his life. She had been in England or Europe when he'd been shot. He hadn't wanted to take her away from her latest young lover, and he knew there would be one. His mother was never without her latest boy toy.

His mother had also been devastated by his father's death. She had, however, chosen to bury her sorrow in working with her charity organization and roaming the planet. While Mason didn't approve of his mother's lifestyle, he reasoned that she did so only to ease the pain of losing his dad.

Mason was looking forward to the visit. He needed someone to talk to and, despite everything, he loved his mother.

She'd make everything all right.

Lianne Thomas entered her office, its vibrancy welcoming her with open arms. Though the room bloomed with shades of yellow and green, hints of earthy-brown prevented it from being too feminine. Instead, the combination of colors created a soothing coolness that never failed to calm her.

She moved to her desk, refusing to acknowledge the stacked in-box brimming with envelopes of various sizes. For a while she sat in silence, disoriented and unsure of what to do next. The six weeks of leave had left her rusty, but the time off had been necessary. Her last case had been a difficult one, but Lianne had the satisfaction of knowing that she'd finally brought a criminal—who had haunted her for years—to justice. The nature of the man's crimes had left her emotionally drained.

Lianne was glad to be back at work and determined to make a dent in several of the files covering her desk. Her time in England with her parents had revived her and, despite their years of estrangement, they'd finally made steps in healing the strained relationship that existed between them. While enjoying the lush English summer, she'd found the time to curl up with the latest release from her favorite romance author, relax and forget the cares of the world that too often threatened to consume her life.

That was one of the reasons she'd decorated the office as she had. Outside, the real world with its evilness and violence made her feel dirty. Inside, her office provided the calm she needed.

It was her paradise, her refuge.

Lianne sat quietly for a moment, glancing at the empty desk across from her. Her partner, Brent, was due back tomorrow. Returning to work a day early had been a good idea. She wanted to be re-acclimatized before he returned. Lianne prided herself on always being prepared, and even though they had been partners for several years, she'd only allowed him in to a very small part of her life.

Well, time to get to work. She flicked her ancient computer on, watching patiently as it scrolled through its labored routine. When the desktop of cluttered icons finally appeared, she logged on to

the internal network and immediately saw a message from Stan. The message was simple. "Come
to my office."

She groaned. Maybe, she shouldn't have come
into the office a day early. Somehow Stan had seen
her enter the building.

Minutes later, Lianne walked briskly along the
corridor leading to Stan Devonish's office, responding to greetings of "Welcome back" with her usual
friendly smile.

When she reached Stan's office, she knocked
gently on the door.

"Come in," came the gruff response. Lianne
smiled, accustomed to his seemingly grumpy dis-
position. She had learned long ago that under his
coarse exterior, Stan was a sweetheart.

When she entered the room, her gaze automatically moved to the two strange men who occupied
two of the three chairs before Stan's desk.

"Welcome back, Thomas. Take a seat. Hope you
had a restful holiday?"

She lowered herself to the empty chair. "Yes, I
did, sir. But I'm glad to be back. Next time I'm going somewhere warmer."

"Well, you'll be happy about your next assignment." He turned to the two men. "Let me introduce
you to Special Agent Aiden Smart and Brian Monroe."

Heads nodded as eyes locked. Then a slow measured assessment of each other.

"Have you heard of the Philip McMaster murder case?"

She turned back to her boss, immediately intrigued. "Yes, isn't Cordoni on trial for having McMaster executed? The trial begins in a few weeks, doesn't it?"

"Two weeks to be exact. And that's where you come in. The star witness, Jason Clarkson, has been in hiding for about three months now…but Cordoni's been trying to get to his wife and son. For now, we have them in a safe house, but we keep having to move them every few days. Cordoni is a powerful man and he'll do anything to stop Clarkson from testifying."

Lianne felt the tingle of excitement she got whenever she was told of a new case.

"So where do I come in?"

"Tomorrow, you'll be leaving for the island of Barbados. You're going to be a nanny to the Clarkson boy, Damien, for the duration of the trial. You're responsible for ensuring nothing happens to Clarkson's wife and the boy.

"Take Smart and Monroe to your office and they'll brief you on the details of the setup. Sorry to have you out of the office so soon, but you did say you wanted some sunshine. Barbados is the perfect place to be at this time of year!" He chuckled, pleased by his attempt at humor.

Hours later, Lianne lay in bed, reading the notes from a folder she'd received during the briefing. Everything about the Cordoni case fascinated her. The session with Smart and Monroe had only confirmed that Jason Clarkson's decision to testify had not only put his life at risk but that of his wife and son. Lianne could not help but admire the courage of such a man.

She immediately liked the two agents assigned to work with her. Aiden Smart, with his quick humor hiding an intelligence far beyond his age, and the quiet Brian Monroe with his eye for detail. She'd been impressed by the witty repartee between the two, and had sensed the strong bond and loyalty. However, she was glad her partner Brent would be joining them in Barbados. Each of the men would be undercover and staying at the same resort.

Lianne lifted a photo of Clarkson's wife and son, studying it carefully for the umpteenth time. Lianne could not help but respond to the loving way Sheila Clarkson's arms wrapped around her small son. The beautiful woman in the photo stared back at Lianne through intelligent eyes, her happiness evident in her smile. There was no doubt about the degree of love she felt for her son.

Lianne had to admit Shelia Clarkson seemed like the kind of woman she would like to know.

Since reading the files, she had come to respect the woman's immense strength of character. Clarkson had been concerned about his family's safety, but Sheila had been the one to convince her husband that testifying was the right thing to do.

Lianne studied the boy, Damien, carefully. The child was all smiles regardless of the fact that his two front teeth were missing. The product of an interracial marriage, he was fortunate to draw his features from the best of both parents. With skin the color of dark caramel and a handsomely charming pair of green eyes, which were so obviously replicas of his father's, Lianne could tell he would break hearts when he was older.

Lianne replaced the photo, closed the folder and placed it on the dresser. She needed to get some sleep. Tomorrow would be a long day. From Ronald Reagan National, they'd have to travel to Miami and then a three-hour flight to Barbados.

She'd visited the island several years ago, so she was looking forward to returning. Of course, this was no holiday, but she hoped she'd get the opportunity to visit some of the island's main attractions.

She smiled.

Playing a nanny would be relatively simple.

Carolyn Sinclair could never be accused of being old. Despite reaching fifty-six a few months ago and refusing to acknowledge the day had actually been on the calendar, she continued to be permanently forty-five, even with a son who had just passed his fortieth birthday.

But Carolyn could afford the little untruth. She could easily pass for forty-five or younger. From the top of her skillfully coiffed hair to her daintily painted toes, she carried her youth like one of the elegant handbags that forever adorned her arm. What gave her added satisfaction and pride was knowing that no part of her well-maintained body was cosmetic.

But today, the concept of age and growing old was the furthest thing from her mind. Today, a day that she'd hoped would never come, her darkest secret was about to be revealed. A secret that could affect her relationship with her son—a son she loved more than life itself.

Tears threatened makeup she had painstakingly put on just before her three-course breakfast. All of which were part of the routine that was Carolyn Sinclair's life.

But the task ahead was not part of her daily routine. Death never was, but Mason needed to know. She could lie to him no longer.

The picture of Joshua Buchanan in the obituary section of the newspaper had forced her to return to the U.S. earlier than planned. She regretted leaving the virile Jean Paul, but when she'd made the decision to tell Mason the truth, she'd boarded the first flight available.

Now, she had to face up to a tiny infraction in her teenage years that threatened the nature of her relationship with her son.

But she knew her son. Mason would been angry for a few days and then he'd assess the situation with the maturity that was so much a part of the boy he'd always been.

Boy? Yes, she still thought of him as her little boy. She remembered the first time she'd held him in her arms and known that she'd made the right decision not to give him up. When he'd opened his eyes for the first time and had seemed to look deep into her soul, she had fallen in love with her son and known she'd do anything to protect him from her past.

And then John Sinclair had come along, taken care of the situation and she'd buried a part of her past until that morning three days ago when it had reared its ugly head.

She knew Mason, but asking him to understand the lies she had told him may be a bit too much for him to handle. Carolyn knew the time had come to tell the truth, whatever the consequences.

Carolyn flowed into the room. His mother never walked or strutted; she flowed.

As always she wore a dress that fitted her to

perfection. She radiated class. Carolyn Sinclair only did things with class. And with a captivated audience, she'd put on a subtle show that highlighted all of her assets—and there were many.

But today something was different. His mother's face did not carry its usual calm sophistication. He knew his mother well. Knew her every mood, her every expression. Today, there was an uncertainty and caution to her usual flow.

Something was wrong.

Maybe she'd broken up with her latest young stud, he wondered. Immediately, he knew it wasn't so.

Maybe she'd fallen in love again.

His speculation was placed on hold when she reached him, bending elegantly to peck him on the cheek.

"Oh, darling, I only heard about your accident a few days ago. I've been staying at a friend's house in the south of France. I'm so sorry. If I had known, I would have come sooner. I did leave some messages on your voice mail, but when you didn't reply I assumed you were on a case. I wonder why Sam didn't try to reach me."

As soon as the words slipped from her mouth, she stopped, immediately realizing the implications of her statement.

She paused, glanced at him and knew. Tears settled in her eyes.

"I'm so sorry, darling. Stupid me. Sam would have called."

She sat on the bed, placing her arms around him, drawing him closer.

For what seems like hours, they sat holding each. Over the years, they'd drifted apart, but there was no doubt in either of their minds that they loved each other. They'd endured too much together. There was no need for those three words to be said, yet they said them often. Carolyn had insisted that caring and affection would be very much a part of their home. For as long as Mason could remember, he'd heard those words pour from her lips.

"Mason, I have something to say to you. This may not be the best time, but it's about time you know." She paused, as if uncertain of what to say. A finger flicked a lock of hair from her eyes.

"Maybe the best way to do this is to show you something." She opened her handbag and searched inside for a while before she withdrew a newspaper clipping and handed it to him.

He took it, curiosity getting the better of him. He glanced at the picture, wondering about the identity of the man in the photo.

And immediately he knew.

He couldn't tell what made him so certain, but he knew that the man was his father.

The man was his father. The words echoed in

his mind. Who was the man he'd just been thinking about?

His mother's husband.

So, this was what his English-literature teacher had meant when she'd tried to teach him the literary term *irony*. He'd always struggled for examples. Ironically, the perfect example had fallen right into his lap.

His mother had a lot of explaining to do.

He placed the clipping on the bed and turned to face her. He wanted to scream, to call her names that she'd taught him never to call anyone.

But somehow, she looked older, afraid. The only time he'd ever seen his mother like this was when she discovered his…father…damn, he didn't even know what to call him…had cancer.

"So, aren't you going to say something?" Her voice was cautious, as if she expected him to be angry.

Yes, he was angry. Mason could feel the heat of his rage boiling deep inside, but somehow, he didn't want her to see his anger.

This must be poetic justice for some sin I committed. He'd seen scenes similar to this on television, but none with quite the originality of his version. *Let's see. The man I thought was my father is dead, but the man who's really my father and who was alive all these years, is also now dead.*

He heard himself laugh, a hollow, empty sound that tore from deep within.

"I'll reserve my anger for after you've told me the whole sordid soap opera of your life."

She jerked as if he'd slapped her. Her face went pale. He'd wanted to hurt her and now that he had, he regretted it. She hadn't brought him up to be cruel.

"I'm sorry. I didn't mean to say that. I don't know what happened so I shouldn't be judge and jury before I hear the evidence."

Again, Carolyn's hand flicked nervously at her hair. He could see the look of sadness in her eyes.

"You loved him. I can see that."

"Yes, I did. But that didn't stop me from loving your father. I grew to love your father more than life itself. You must know that."

"I do, I'm sorry. I'm just so confused. You're saying 'your father' and I'm not even sure who you mean. I don't know what I mean."

"I met him when we moved to Brooklyn while I was still in high school. I was just fifteen and he was a senior." Her voice was whimsical. He could feel her memories.

"He was in New York staying with family for the summer and planning to study on the West Coast. He was from a fairly well-off family, but my mother had plans for me to marry a white man. Says it would help to raise our status. I knew she'd never approve of a man who wanted to be a missionary.

But I fell in love with him anyway and then I discovered I was pregnant. He disappeared and I didn't even get a chance to tell him. His grandmother told me he'd returned home to Chicago and she didn't know how to get in contact with him. The picture of him in the paper is the first time I've seen him in all these years."

She paused, as if needing the interruption to regain control.

"So I understand from the article that I have brothers?"

"Yes, three brothers."

She paused, hesitant about what else to say.

He didn't mind, not wanting to hear much more. Instead he changed the subject.

"I'm thinking about leaving the Bureau."

"You are?" She looked at him strangely. There was disbelief in her voice. She'd never truly warmed to the idea of his being an agent. Of course, she had larger dreams for him. Politics or law or even medicine.

Of course, *no* had been her answer when, at sixteen years old, he'd told her his dream.

But she'd changed her mind, as he'd known she would.

His mother may try to live up to the status quo, but she would never have killed his dream. When she'd eventually accepted the inevitable, she'd supported him with the same fervor as if it were her own dream.

"I shouldn't be surprised. I've known for quite awhile, you've not been happy. Sam, too. But I knew you'd tell me when you were ready."

There was silence.

He didn't want to talk anymore. He wanted to be alone.

"Well, my darling. I have to go. Let's not talk about any more of this now. I'm going to go over and see Clair. I'll take her shopping. Get her out of the house."

"Thanks, Mom."

"Yes, and please forgive me. I should have told you about your father years ago, but the time never seemed right."

With that she hugged him again, placing one of her delicate kisses on his cheek.

"I love you, sweetheart."

"I love you, too, Mom," Mason responded.

Carolyn flowed from the room.

Mason gripped the cane, moving slowly toward the window. Outside, the lights of the Manhattan skyline flickered and glowed, illuminating the busyness of the night despite the late hour. He could not sleep, but this time thoughts of what his mother had told him filled his troubled mind.

Brothers?

Three?

Anger burned inside, but already curiosity had him wondering about his brothers...and his father.

He glanced at the folder again, wanting to take another look, but knowing that the man reminded him too much of himself with the same dark caramel complexion, the same brandy-colored eyes, the same quirky smile with the single dimple that never failed to appear.

He closed his eyes, trying to conjure an image of his other father, but each time the picture faded to be replaced by a face that seemed to be already engraved on his mind's eye.

He no longer felt angry with his mother. Just an overwhelming sense of sadness for the young girl who'd been forced to give up her childhood to raise her son, without the approval or blessings of her parents.

The idea flashed in his mind once, and then a second time. He knew what he needed to do. He had contacts in the Bureau. People he only had to call on to do a special task and they would without hesitation. He wanted to find out as much as possible about his brothers.

They held a knowledge of his heritage and who he was. It felt strange after all these years of being a confident ambitious go-getter who'd known a family history that was no longer the real one. It was almost as if the person he had been no longer existed. Yes, he was a Sinclair by name, but the Buchanan blood flowed in his veins and he needed to know what that meant.

Mason Buchanan.

He spoke the name, enjoying the sound and feel of it as it rolled off his tongue.

Confidence and *strength* were two words that the name possessed. He turned from the window abruptly, and his knees buckled with the strain of the movement. He landed with a soft thud on the floor.

For minutes he sat there, willing the pain to subside. Then slowly, he raised himself. He hopped to the bed, collapsing on it.

When was this going to stop?

He hated being crippled. He hated the word, but he didn't feel *physically challenged.* He just felt *crippled.*

For hours he just lay there, his thoughts troubled by the events that had unraveled today and his future. Already he was weeks ahead of today. As soon as he was out of here, he was going to find his brothers.

Chapter 2

Carolyn lifted the cover of the chest she stored in the attic. In it lay her wedding dress, a mass of ivory lace that she had worn when she'd married John Sinclair. Tears came to her eyes at the thought of the man who had once loved her and given her years of happiness and contentment. This time, however, the dress did not hold her interest. Instead, she removed a tiny jewelry box from beneath the gown, where she had carefully placed it over twenty years ago.

Sitting, she opened the box, her heart skipping a beat when she saw the object of her search. With trembling hands she removed a discolored photo, holding it with care. Her eyes focused on the image of the young man who'd stolen her fragile heart and then had left her alone to endure the wrath and scorn of her parents.

Though she'd been angry and hurt, she'd suspected her parents had something to do with Joshua's disappearance. She didn't know what hold they'd had over him back then, but she knew the kind of power her mother had exerted. The fact that he'd never tried to contact Carolyn still pained her.

She had never been more shocked than when she'd opened the newspaper a few weeks ago to see his face staring up at her with the same piercingly hypnotic eyes that she saw each time she looked at her son. Years ago, those same eyes had drawn her in with their intensity, weakening her until she could no longer resist his charm.

When Mason had been released from the hospital two days ago, she'd immediately left for her home in New Jersey. Like a magnet, the contents of the chest drew her with its memories.

Memories she'd tried to bury over the years. But vivid images of the past continued to surface at the most unexpected times.

Carolyn could still remember clearly the first time she'd met Joshua. She'd just arrived in the city, a shy unassuming teenager, angered by her parents' decision to move to New York. The drab streets of Brooklyn contrasted with the serenity of the streets of the tiny town where she'd grown up and made her yearn for the familiarity of her childhood home.

That was…until she'd met him.

Joshua Robert Buchanan.

And her life had changed forever….

The soulful voices of the members of the Brooklyn Gospel Hall Choir filled the church with their sweetness and passion. Carolyn's discomfort continued to increase. A stranger to the city, she had been dragged to church by her mother, but she would have preferred to stay at home. Her mother, however, had immediately thrown herself into the life of the community by joining its most visible church.

A month had passed since arriving in Brooklyn and Carolyn missed her friends more and more with each passing day. Her anger at her mother continued to threaten their already fragile relationship. Letting her father know how she felt was a waste of time. Yes, he was a strong, strapping man, but her mother could easily reduce him to a bumbling fool. Carolyn couldn't blame him. Her mother was just too overpowering a personality.

And then *he* had walked in, his swagger leisurely, as if *he* didn't have a care in the world. He was tall and slim with his hair in a short Afro, not unlike the one her father wore, but definitely not the full Afro worn by all the followers of the current black-power movement. He was handsome, a fact highlighted by the smile and laughter with which he greeted members of the choir.

When he sat next to her, Carolyn wondered why, but realized that of the people in the church not practicing with the choir, she was the only one around his age. Her heart quickened and she tried to avoid looking in his direction.

After a few moments of silence, he turned to her. "Hi, I'm Joshua…. Most people call me Robert, but I prefer Joshua. He's one of my favorite characters from the Bible."

He held out his hand.

When she touched him in response, she drew her hand back quickly, shocked by the heat she felt.

She looked up at him, seeing the same awareness in his eyes.

"Didn't expect that, did you?" he whispered boldly.

"No, I didn't." She couldn't believe what she'd just said. Her words seemed brazen and not in keeping with her usual sense of propriety. Her mother had taught her that good girls didn't flirt.

"I knew you'd be special the moment I walked in and saw you sitting there." His voice was a mere whisper, yet soft and sexy.

"What's your name?"

"Carolyn."

"A perfect name for someone so beautiful."

"Don't you have any respect? You're in church!"

"Yes, I am. But can you think of a better place for me to tell you how I feel about you? God has always taught me to be honest. So are you going to let me kiss you?

"Nothing to say?" he asked after she remained silent.

"No, nothing to say. You seem to have everything all worked out."

"Come, let's leave here. Let your mother know we're going to the ice-cream shop around the corner. No, let me tell her. Go get your coat and meet me by the door."

He moved quickly, said something to her mother and smiled, the perfect gentleman. Her mother glanced in her direction and smiled in response, approval in her expression.

Joshua returned, waited for her to stand and then put his hand in hers.

That night Carolyn felt the tender touch of a man's kiss for the first time.

And she fell hopelessly and completely in love.

Mason placed the pictures on the desk for the third time since he'd received them in the mail that morning. He was pleased with the information the private investigator had been able to accumulate in the short time since he'd hired him. He wanted to know and remember as much about his brothers as possible.

It had taken all of his willpower to refrain from calling one of the three phone numbers he now had at his disposal. He still could not believe that he had four brothers. Three in fact, since one, the youngest, had passed away several years ago.

He placed his hand on the picture of his oldest brother, Patrick, who, at thirty-nine, lived in Illinois, was married and had no children. He was an accountant and his wife, Paula, a research analyst.

His brother Taurean was the most interesting. He lived in Barbados and ran a resort on the island with his wife, Alana, and his stepdaughter, Melissa. Mason had even discovered that Taurean had spent seven years in prison for the mercy killing of their youngest brother, Corey.

The final brother was Daniel, the preacher, who lived in Philadelphia, was married and had a son who'd just turned one.

Mason found it interesting that each of his brothers looked so alike...and so much like him. He realized he was probably the smallest of his father's children. He favored his mother in that respect. Yes, he was not of a large stature like his brothers, but

there was strength and power in his leanness that surprised many a criminal when they underestimated
his lethal ability. The lighter shade of his complexion and the curliness of his hair lessened the resemblance. His eyes, the same brandy color, however,
also bore the same intensity as his brothers'.

Mason wondered what he should do with all the
information he'd acquired.

Who was he fooling?

He already knew he was going to Barbados. Not
only would it be the perfect place to recuperate
from his injury, but he could use the time to decide
what he wanted to do with his life. It would also be
the perfect opportunity to get to know one of his
brothers. He was still unsure if he wanted to let
them know of his existence.

He lifted the cordless phone from the table and
punched in the number of the travel agency he
often used.

"Good morning, Travel World, how may I help
you?"

"Cheryl, this is Mason Sinclair. I want to book
a flight to Barbados to leave in a few days. Let me
see—" he glanced at the calendar just above the
desk "—that's the twenty-third. Can you also book
me a reservation at the Sunrise Resort? I want to
stay for a month," he said in a rush of words.

"Okay Mason, take your time. Can you run that

information by me again? But slower this time." He heard the humor in her voice.

He repeated the information and was about to say goodbye when her professional voice changed to a seductive whisper.

"So, Mason, I haven't seen you in months. How about dinner tonight at my place?" she asked hopefully.

"Sorry, I've been pretty busy planning this trip to Barbados. Maybe I'll give you a call when I get back," Mason said, unwilling to make any promises. Cheryl was all about sex, and right now, sex was the last thing on his mind. "For now, just e-mail me the arrangements when they're ready, okay?"

Mason put the receiver down before she could respond, not wanting to discuss his decision. He had other things on his mind.

What filled his every waking hour was the news his mother had given him. At first he'd decided to leave the situation as it was, but when he'd received the dossier on his brothers, he'd started to see it as more that just a folder of facts and statistics, but of men with the same blood running through their veins. There were so many things he wanted to know about his brothers…and his father.

Mason picked up the phone again. He didn't want to tell his mother his plans, but he couldn't keep something like this from her, and she'd be worried if she didn't hear from him when she called. Despite his anger, he still loved her, and she was the only one who knew what had happened those many years ago.

Carolyn's voice came over the line, formal and businesslike. "Sorry, I am not at home at the moment. If you wish me to contact you, please leave a message after the beep. Of course, I'll return the call as soon as humanly possible. Thank you."

Mason sighed with relief, glad she was not at home. Despite the inevitability of letting her know of his plan, he preferred to deal with her questions at a later date. Now, he'd leave a brief message on the phone letting her know he was going to Barbados.

Laying the phone on the bed, he picked up the pictures again for one final glance before he placed them back in the envelope, the need to remember, sudden and compelling. He rose slowly to his feet, stifling the groan of pain at the stiffness in his leg. He reached for his cane and struggled from the room, hating not only the restrictions that his injury placed on him, but the feeling of helplessness that tried its best to make him crazy.

Mason moved sluggishly along the corridor to the place in the house that held strong memories of his "other" father. The den, filled with items from his childhood, was the only place where memories of his dad were still vivid and real. The room had become his sanctuary, a place where he could sit and relax when he needed to talk.

When Mason entered the room, he moved immediately to the large sofa. His dad had loved that ragged broken-down relic. Many a night, Mason had watched him fall asleep in the sofa with the day's newspaper in his hands. Mason smiled at the familiar memory of his mother bending to kiss his dad before waking him and demanding that he go upstairs to his bed.

Mason had sat in the same den often, doing his homework while his father had sat working on some project or another for the office. In this same room, his dad had taught him to love the printed word. Rows and rows of shelves still overflowed with books he'd inherited from his father as well as those he'd added over the years. He'd loved this man with all the love he had. It hurt to know that John Sinclair was not his biological father, but there was no doubt in his mind that the man had loved him as if he were his own son.

For a moment Mason could almost see him, his eyes twinkling with humor. His father's laughter had been infectious; a deep rumble that exploded into a loud uninhibited expression of happiness. John Sinclair had enjoyed life to the fullest and when he'd taken ill and cancer had ravished his body, he'd never given up the laughter, closing his eyes for the final time with a smile on his face.

It was times like these that Mason missed his father most. He felt the sting of tears, but refused to give in to the unexpected wave of emotion.

All that had been his past and his heritage was only a figment of his imagination. A lie that threatened his identity and sense of belonging, leaving him feeling disoriented and…lost. Maybe it was wrong to feel this way, but he had no control over the current situation, which had placed him in a constant state of unrest.

He was torn between love for his mother and dad and the need to do something to find out who he was. He wanted to know his brothers, his biological father, his grandparents and all those who bore the Buchanan name.

He was not sure what his future held. Maybe he wouldn't like what he discovered, but at least he'd have satisfied his curiosity.

He closed his eyes, willing the presence of the man with whom he'd shared many private moments.

Tonight, however, the image appeared but slowly faded to be replaced by another face with eyes so intense they could see his soul.

Lianne closed her eyes, inhaling the freshness of the warm tropical breeze. All she'd heard about the island was true. Its vibrant beauty still left her in awe each time she ventured outdoors. The island's greenness and the vivid colors of its flora complemented the golden sunshine and azure skies. Lianne felt as if she were in paradise.

She watched as Damien leaped along the beach, occasionally stopping to examine whatever caught his interest. They had arrived at the resort about two weeks ago and the boy remained quiet and reserved, ignoring her attempts to be friendly. Only his mother and his daily romps on the beach seemed able to draw the occasional smile.

Lianne glanced in Sheila Clarkson's direction, knowing that the pages of the book the silent brooding woman held in her hands still remained unread. Initially, Lianne had wondered at the woman's ability to adapt to her current situation, since she seemed unmoved by what was happening. That was until Lianne had heard her crying one night and realized that the book she held in her hand was the one she'd held for the past two weeks.

At times, when Sheila felt she was alone, Lianne would see her staring off into the distance, her face carrying lines of anguish that disappeared as soon as she felt someone watching her.

At other times, Lianne saw her quickly glance at the television when the international-news segment of the local news show was in session.

Back in the U.S., the case was moving slowly.

Jury selection, a long and laborious exercise, had finally been completed and the case was now in its first week. Even now, Lianne was fascinated by the case and logged on to the Internet every night to follow its progress.

But she didn't want to think of any of that now. She just wanted to bask in the sun and lose some of the paleness she'd acquired in England. Already her skin was regaining some of its normally healthy glow, though she'd applied a liberal amount of sunscreen to ensure she did not burn.

In the distance, a seagull screamed and Lianne glanced in its direction, watching as it soared gracefully before swooping down to skillfully catch a fish in its beak.

A cold wind caused her to shiver. No, she had no intention of being paranoid. The Clarksons were safe. Everything possible had been done to ensure the secrecy of her charges' whereabouts. She had no intention of letting anything happen to them. Several times before, she'd worked with witness protection, and each time there'd been no leaks. She had every intention of making sure her record remain unblemished.

She continued to watch as Damien chased after a crab, which quickly disappeared into its hole.

And then she saw *him*. A guest who'd only arrived at the resort a few days ago. From the moment she'd seen him, she'd experienced that unexpected tug of attraction.

Yesterday, she'd finally met him.

He had literally barreled himself into her life. She'd been on the way to her room after using one of the resort's phone booths when she'd crashed into a solid wall of muscle. She'd watched in shock as he'd fallen to the floor, his groan of agony heartwrenching and unexpected. She'd spotted the cane that had rolled along the floor, realizing she must have seriously hurt him.

Embarrassed, Lianne had reached for the cane and then turned to him, wanting to make sure she'd not caused any permanent damage.

"I'm sorry. I didn't mean to make you fall." She'd watched as he'd tried to struggle to his feet. She'd held her hand out, but he'd refused to take it, instead grasping the cane and slowly righting himself.

"I'm sorry," he'd finally said. "It's my fault. I wasn't looking where I was going."

Lianne couldn't respond; instead she'd found herself staring into two of the most beautiful eyes she'd ever seen on a man. They were the color of pale brandy, an unusual color for a black man, but somehow they seemed perfect for him.

He'd smiled, a slow sensual revealing of his soul that had drawn her in with its promise.

Lianne had watched as he'd limped painfully

away, and then he was gone, leaving her standing there with her heart pounding rapidly in her chest.

Amazed by her reaction, she'd attempted to force his image from her mind, but the intensity of his eyes was still vivid and real. For the past few years she had been so focused on her career and her advancement in the organization that love and romance had taken the proverbial back seat. Not that she cared too much, since her brushes with love and romance had only left her cynical about the so-called happily-ever-after.

But something had attracted her to the stranger from the moment she'd seen him. Each evening, he walked the beach, his movements slow and labored, but she admired the strength of his determination. After his walk, he'd sit on a large bolder overlooking the sea and she would wonder what had brought him to the island and what could have possibly made him so sad.

On several occasions, Lianne had almost made an attempt to speak to him, but had decided against it. She didn't want any distractions, especially in light of her current mission. She wanted to be focused wholly and solely on the Clarksons.

As if demonstrating her resolve, Lianne turned to the little boy who seemed engrossed with something on the sand. She rose, determined to befriend the boy who continued to hold her at arms' length. No, she needed to think of him as Damien.

When she reached him, he looked up, his eyes pooled with their usual wariness. She glanced down and saw a large crab, its claw ready for battle.

"I want to hold it, but it'll hurt me." She was surprised he spoke.

Lianne saw her chance. She carefully placed her right hand over the crab's back and with lightning speed grasped it, her hand away from the frantically waving claws.

Damien looked at her in awe, admiration replacing the wariness.

"How did you do that?"

"It's simple. You just have to make sure you put your hands around the back so the claws can't reach your hands. But maybe we should leave the crab and let it go home. It has to be scared about all that is happening." She put the crab down and it scurried away.

"Scared of us," he responded, as if he couldn't imagine why a crab would be afraid of them.

"Remember the crab is really small and to the crab we're really big…. It's just putting its claws up to protect itself because it is scared."

Damien was quiet for a while, as if contemplating the logic of what she'd said.

"You're really smart…and brave."

"Thank you! But promise me you won't try to do it when no one's around. You may get hurt if you try without practice."

Again, he was silent. "Okay, I promise."

"So how'd you like to go swimming with me?"

"I can't swim."

"Want me to teach you? I'll ask your mum."

He hesitated, glancing at the wide expanse of water. "Okay, I'd like to learn. Thank you for asking me."

She held out her hand and he took it.

Lianne smiled. Finally, she'd made the breakthrough she'd wanted.

As they walked toward his mother, she saw a movement to her left. She turned, seeing the intriguing stranger, and for the briefest of moments their gazes locked, and then he looked away, but not before Lianne recognized the spark of awareness that flamed.

Mason watched as the woman and child walked toward the other woman who spent the majority of her time reading. For the most part, she seemed oblivious of the boy, who spent his time roaming the beach looking for what treasures he could salvage.

Every day, Mason watched them as they found their way to the beach in the late afternoon—an odd trio, the boy and reader obviously mother and son; the other, probably the boy's nanny. Though the boy bore little physical resemblance to his mother, his mannerisms often mimicked hers—the way he held his head while concentrating on whatever caught his attention was a characteristic he shared with his mother as she read her book, or when she was obviously lost in thought.

However, something didn't feel right. Initially, Mason had wondered if the women were lovers, but had rejected that notion almost immediately. A wall of tension stood between the two women, creating a distance that was obvious to the trained eye. What existed between them was not sexual. He could bet his life on it. But something was definitely not right.

The nanny, especially, intrigued him. With skin the shade of soft caramel, she was beautiful. Not in the traditional sense of the word, since she carried herself in a simple non-glamorous way, but he had noticed a lot about her the day they'd crashed into each other. And yes, there was something about her that didn't ring true. He wasn't sure what was wrong, but there was something; he just couldn't put his finger on at the moment.

Mason watched the gentle sway of her hips and experienced the now familiar surge of desire he felt each time he saw her.

They stopped in front of the boy's mother and the nanny bent to say something to her. She turned to the boy and he pulled his shirt off.

Then the nanny slipped from the robe she wore. Mason stopped breathing.

She wore a modest one-piece that did nothing to hide the firm, luscious curves no nanny he knew of could have. This was a woman who had the kind of body that could only be the result of working out regularly.

She continued to baffle him with her ambiguity and if he had been on holiday, he'd have satisfied his curiosity.

She took the boy's hand and together they ran to the water's edge. Mason's eyes protested, disappointed at her inevitable entry into the water. For the next half hour, however, he watched as they frolicked and played in the gentle surf.

When they exited the water, he saw her glance in his direction and nod, her eyes hidden by the shadow of the sun. The boy's mother joined them and they disappeared in the direction of the resort's main building.

Soon, the beach was empty. In the next half an hour he would go on his evening walk along the beach. The therapist had emphasized that a daily stroll on the sand could help to strengthen his leg, and already he could feel the soreness that came with frequent exercise. He knew that he needed to slow down but he felt driven into the habit of walking mornings and evenings, despite the therapist's words of caution.

His thoughts moved to his brother. Already he was impressed with the tall man who looked so much like him. Mason had been careful to ensure that he wore dark shades at all times, not wanting to give rise to any questions. He knew he was being a bit paranoid, but he could not help it.

On the day he'd arrived, a few weeks ago, Taurean's pregnant wife, Alana, had glanced at him, her gaze lingering for the briefest of moments, but her curiosity had quickly been replaced by a friendly smile when she'd officially welcomed him to the resort.

During his first few days on the island, he had discovered she was an artist. Several of her paintings of local scenes hung along the corridors of the resort. One particularly spectacular sunrise hung in the foyer, a masterpiece of serenity with an army of birds dancing as if a part of some intricate aerial ballet.

Mason could tell his brother and his wife were very much in love. The way they looked at each other, the stolen kisses when they thought no one was looking and the apparent need to touch each other were obvious testaments to the fact.

Their daughter, Melissa, was a delight. He'd seen her and twin girls racing on the beach. She seemed to be about ten-years-old, and was a bundle of energy, always running and laughing, never staying still for a moment. There were other times when he'd seen Melissa pensively sitting in the balcony of a house off from the main resort.

Sometimes, she'd been reading and at other times he'd seen her with a sketch pad, intent on creating her own masterpieces.

He supposed the girl had some of her mother's talent and suspected she would grow up to be a talented artist as well.

But there would always be laughter, a warm bubbly sound that floated with the wind, caressing him with its coolness.

He glanced in the direction of the ocean, realizing darkness had fallen. In the distance, the lights from several fishing boats twinkled with the movement of the waves.

Soon, the moon would appear in all its splendor, caressing the island with its rays of purest white. The nights in Barbados had quickly become his favorite time of day. It was then that the island's creatures came alive. He had recently seen the movie *Ray* and found himself fascinated by the concept of heightened senses. He'd started to enjoy listening, just shutting his other senses out and hearing the music of the island.

He closed his eyes, willing himself to hear the sounds around him. The splash of the waves, the whisper of the winds through the trees, the cooing of a dove and...

In the distance a dog barked, and he laughed. It must be the mongrel dog he saw roaming the beach every day. The dog seemed to have no owner, instead eating scraps it found on the sand. Mason had tried to call him, a dangerous move, but he felt some strange attachment to the animal whose wary eyes reflected his own sense of mistrust and betrayal.

He heard a scuffling sound and opened his eyes. The dog stood a mere ten meters away. The light from one of the lamps that dotted the beach allowed him to see the animal clearly.

The two stared at one another for several moments until Mason broke the standoff by returning his attention to the sea. He would not go walking tonight, he decided, opting instead to sit and enjoy the night. He was surprised when, hours later, he rose, finding the dog lying at his feet fast asleep.

Mason smiled and attempted to stretch his hands out, but pulled them back. He remembered, as a child, his dad telling him that dreams were stored in the moon and that you had to be willing to reach out and embrace the moonlight to hold your dreams.

Fanciful thinking.

Dreams were for kids who didn't know any better. He had no intention of being a kid anymore.

The man picked the phone up, his hand trembling, anticipating the voice that would continue to

make demands on him. He'd thought it would stop
with the previous call, but the calls had continued.
There was nothing he could do at this point. He was
already too deep into the whole sordid situation. He
needed to get the information or else his own family's life would be in danger.

Just a few more days and he should have the information the man needed.

When he finally dialed the phone, it was answered on the first ring.

"You have the information for me?"

Was that all? No *hello* or *good morning?* The
man needed a serious lesson in etiquette.

"No," he answered reluctantly. "But I'm close to
finding out. I'll have the information to you soon.
I promise." He cringed, hearing the desperation in
his voice. The man had reduced him to a wimp.
He'd been head of an important organization but
had transformed into this. He was pathetic and
spineless, but he had to protect his family.

He had no choice.

All he hoped was that the leak wouldn't lead to
him.

He just had to be very careful.

Chapter 3

Mason pressed the button for the elevator and waited patiently for it to arrive. When the door parted, his heart skipped a beat. His niece stood there, a broad smile on her face.

He stepped inside, returning the smile but unsure of what to say to her. He didn't have much experience with children; didn't like them too much either. There was something intimidating about this little girl who always looked so happy and full of life.

"Hi." Her voice was filled with laughter.

"Hi," he responded.

"I'm Melissa Buchanan. What's your name?"

"I'm Mason Sinclair."

She hesitated for a moment. "I'm sorry, I didn't mean to be nosy. My mom always says that I'm too in-quis-itive. But it's fun trying to remember the names of all the people staying in the resort. My dad says I have a good memory, and I'm the one he has to turn to when he wants the name of one of the guests."

She paused for a moment as if formulating what she wanted to say next.

"How did you hurt your leg?" she asked. He heard genuine curiosity and concern in her voice.

"In an accident."

"Does it hurt a lot?"

"Sometimes, but it has been hurting less since I came to Barbados."

The elevator came to a stop and the door opened. He waited for her to exit before following.

"Where're you going?" she asked. "I'm going down to the beach. I can't go in the water. My dad's really busy and my mom's gone to our beach house in Christ Church to paint. I'm going looking for shells. You want to come?"

His immediate reaction was to say no, but he had nothing better to do than sit brooding on the sand. Maybe he needed to be around someone who'd cheer him up.

"Yes, if you're sure you don't mind the company."

"Oh, I don't mind. It's been so boring the past few days. My mom won't be back until next week. She's gone to finish a painting she's doing for a client. And my best friends have gone to Trinidad for the weekend."

"Your best friends? The twin girls?"

"Yes, Kerry and Karen. You've seen me with them." She smiled and then in a very mature voice said, "They're a handful, but Auntie Bertha says I'm the sta-bil-iz-ing influence and the one with the level head. I'm not sure what she means, but it's probably because I'm the smart one."

Mason laughed, his chuckle joining her sweet giggle.

When they reached the path at the back of the resort leading to the beach, Melissa raced down the steps and then halted abruptly. She waited as Mason followed her, his movement slow and labored.

"I'm sorry, we should have left by the other entrance. I hope you didn't hurt yourself?"

"No, I'm fine."

The pain, in fact, was excruciating, but he couldn't admit that to her. He didn't even want to admit it to himself.

"So where're we going for these shells? You must have a large collection by now. I've seen you on the beach."

"Yes, I've been collecting since we came to the island. My best friends and I make all sorts of things. My mom has even sold some of our jewelry chains in the gift shop on the compound."

"So you're talented like your mom."

"Yes, my dad always says I'm going to be a great artist like my mom. She has won numerous awards!" Melissa said, pride in her voice. "Can you draw, too?"

He laughed. "No, definitely not. I'm the worst artist in the world."

She giggled, the sound innocent and refreshing. "But I'm sure there are things you like to do. I love to draw and paint, but I also love the beach and swimming, too."

"Of course, they're things I like to do." He didn't intend to expand, but she looked at him with her clear, honest eyes. He'd not seen eyes so devoid of cynicism in years. Maybe not spending time around children had taken its toll on him. "I like…"

Before he could continue, she shouted, her voice filled with excitement. "Look, look, there's that dog that's always running on the beach. My dad has tried to catch him, but he's too smart. He keeps running away. We'd take him to the vet so we can take care of him, but he seems to prefer to be on his own."

Mason glanced in the direction of the mongrel, knowing it was the dog that had rested at his feet the other night, but still he wasn't sure how wise it would be for her to try to befriend the dog.

On sensing their presence, the dog stopped its play, stood still and stared at them with wary eyes. He barked once and raced off.

"Maybe it's not safe to get too close to him," Mason cautioned.

"Yes, that's what my dad says, but I know he's not going to hurt me. He just needs a friend. I bring food scraps for him all the time. When I first saw him on the beach, he was bleeding. I'm sure his owner used to beat him and that's why he ran away. He just needs to learn to trust people again."

Mason could not help but be amazed at his niece's maturity. But what she said was so true. He was quite aware of the problems that a lack of trust could create in a person's life. For years, he'd trusted his mother. A simple lie—or should he say *omission*—and every aspect of his history had changed forever. The boy he'd been and the man he was—only a lie.

Shaking himself from thoughts that continued to plague him, Mason realized they'd finally reached the water's edge, when Melissa slipped from her slippers, holding them in her hands. Mason followed suit.

"You remind me of my dad and his brothers. You're big like they are. Not *as* big, but big. You have eyes like them, too." Melissa said this with the innocence of a child, not realizing the truth of what she said.

Before he could respond, he heard a shout coming from the direction of the resort. A tiny woman was moving at lightning pace and waving in their direction.

"Auntie Bertha! Auntie Bertha, you're back!" Melissa screamed. She raced to the woman and hurled herself into her arms.

The "Auntie Bertha" held Melissa and kissed her on the cheeks.

"So did you miss me?" Melissa asked.

"Of course, how could I not miss my favorite girl? Your dad says you can spend the night at my home. So are you coming over and see what I brought back for you?"

Melissa squealed. "Yes, yes, let's go right now." And then she turned, as if she suddenly remembered Mason. "I can't go now, Auntie Bertha. Mr. Sinclair promised to help me look for shells. It'll be rude for me to leave him."

Mason laughed. "Melissa, it's fine. You go along and get your gifts. I'm sure there'll be other times to collect shells." And then he turned to the woman.

"Sorry about that. I'm Mason Sinclair. I'm staying at the resort."

For a while she stared at him as if assessing his suitability to be with Melissa and then she smiled.

"I'm Bertha Gooding." For the briefest of moments she hesitated, her gaze intent as if she were looking into his soul. She stretched out her hand. "It's a pleasure to meet you. For some reason you look familiar, but who knows, you may have family on the island."

She paused as if trying to catch her breath. "I'm a friend of the family. Since you're Melissa's friend, I'll invite you to dinner one night, but today we girls have some catching up to do. I have all my New York stuff to unpack and try on. Melissa, I brought you some clothes and the iPod you requested."

Melissa screamed with excitement. "Let's go. Let's go, Auntie Bertha."

"Okay, okay, we'll go soon," she reassured. Bertha turned to Mason. "I'm sorry to take Melissa away from you." Her eyes remained focused on him. "Enjoy the rest of your evening."

"I will, Mrs. Gooding. And Melissa, have fun. We can look for shells another day."

With that, they turned and headed in the direction of the resort.

Mason watched as they walked away, surprised at the unexpected rush of loneliness that gripped him, a far from comfortable feeling.

Carolyn climbed into her 1990 Toyota Corolla, slipped into the driver's seat and closed her eyes, her body relaxing for the first time in hours. Her day of charity work had been exhausting but her sense of duty did not permit her to miss her weekly session at the children's home where she'd been volunteering for the past ten years when she wasn't roaming the European continent.

She wanted to remain at home, ignited by the anger that she felt to the core of her being. What Mason was doing had more than upset her. She couldn't understand why he'd want to go to Barbados. He was only going to stir a hornet's nest.

But she'd been silly to expect him not to do something about what she'd told him. Mason was the son she'd raised and she knew him better than most people, and that didn't mean she could influence him. At no time in his youth had Mason ever listened to her, preferring to take his own path and learn from his mistakes.

She opened her eyes, turned the engine on and pulled out of the parking lot. She took the usual road, hoping that its familiarity would help to ease her troubled mind. Her destination was her special place. The place where she came when life took a turn that she didn't like. She could count the number of times that the park's calm serenity and naturalness had comforted her.

She switched the radio on, pressing the button for her favorite station, and immediately the rich vocals of the late Karen Carpenter filled the car's interior.

Ironically, as Karen sang, the words of the song made her smile. "Rainy Days and Mondays" did always seem to get people down. At least one part of the song was true. Today, Monday, she was definitely not feeling on top of the world, but it was far from being rainy.

She switched the station, in the mood for something a bit lighter. Ah, Whitney Houston's "I Wanna Dance with Somebody" was perfect to ease her from her unusual mood.

In fact, the sun shone in all its glory. Birds flew overhead, and as she pulled into the parking lot, the sound of the lake beckoned her with its gentle whisper.

She parked and quickly slipped from the car, careful to lock it. Her last time here, she had returned to a car empty of several of her personal belongings and the few dollars she kept in case of an emergency. Fortunately, there had been nothing of importance to steal.

She took the familiar path to the north of the parking lot, her usual brown bag of bread in her hands. The ducks would be hungry at this time of day, but she hoped there were no overzealous critters to chase her like on one of her visits earlier this year. She'd run as fast as she could with the flapping of wings behind her, but had quickly dropped the bag and continued to her car. Now, the memory brought laughter, but then she'd been so embarrassed. Especially when she'd lost a heel.

She breathed a sigh of release when the bench she usually sat on was bare of any intruders. To the left, a couple sat, oblivious to their surroundings, more intent on keeping their lips locked.

She sat on the bench and for a while she watched the couple. A deep ache gnawed deep inside. She missed the intimacy of being in love. Yes, she'd had lovers, but in all her life she'd only loved twice.

Joshua and John.

Often at night she'd wake, her body bathed in sweat from her dreams of John. Joshua had been her first love, but John, the man she'd married, had taught her the pleasures of making love. Where Joshua had been innocent and youthful, John had been a man of experience and a skilled lover. Lovemaking between them had never been boring. As a result, very few of her lovers lived up to expectation. Most were now pleasant but unremarkable memories.

The quacking of the ducks drew her from her musing and she opened the bag, tossing its contents in the direction of the hungry birds.

Immediately, they gobbled up their gift, glancing at her with anticipation, but moving on quickly when they realized she had nothing else to offer.

In the distance, fluffy white clouds danced across the sky, but caused no obstruction to the sun's rays. The day was beautiful, and brought memories of a time long gone but one that still lingered in her mind....

Carolyn closed the door behind her, her heart moving at a rate not normal. But tonight was not a normal night. She was meeting Joshua at the soda shop just around the block. She'd told her mother she was going to the cinema with several of her friends from school. Despite that first night when her mother had allowed her to go with Joshua, things had changed. She couldn't understand why her mother didn't want her with Joshua. She'd laid the law down without any explanation.

But the love between the two teenagers was already so intense that to stay away from each other was impossible. Joshua was the most important thing in her life.

Carolyn walked quickly, her feet anticipating the moment she'd see the boy who made her tremble under his gaze.

When she turned the corner on Jay Street, he stood there, his eyes focused on the spot where he knew she'd appear. He moved immediately toward her.

On reaching her, he held her hands and in his eyes she could see the desire. Her lips tingled. She

wanted to feel his lips on her. Kissing him gave rise
to a warm pleasure deep within her that she ached
to experience whenever she saw him. It was as if her
body had a mind of its own and she no longer had
control.

"You look beautiful," he said. His heat warmed
her.

"You, too," she responded.

He chuckled. "Men don't look beautiful."

"Well, to me you do," she teased. "My beautiful
man."

"Okay, let's agree to disagree," he said, his voice
husky with humor.

"So where are we going?" she asked.

"Let's stop and get burgers and milk shakes
then we'll go to the park. There's a free gospel
concert tonight. Hope you like Andraé Crouch
and the Disciples."

Her screams of delight were enough of an answer, before he took her hand and lead her in the
direction of the McDonald's around the corner.

After purchasing two packs of the largest fries
and the largest shakes on sale, they headed in the
direction of the park.

Fifteen minutes later they wormed their way
through the crowd until they found a gentle incline
under a large tree. Joshua spread his jacket on the
ground and sat, motioning for Carolyn to sit between

his legs. She smiled, enjoying the warm feeling that bubbled inside. When she sat, he immediately pulled her gently against him, resting her back against his chest and placing his arms around her.

For a while they sat quietly listening to the music that filled them with its sweet gospel rhythms. Sometimes she sang along with the familiar tunes, at other times she hummed, feeling warm inside when Joshua whispered sweet words in her ears.

A few hours later as they walked toward the cinema where she was to meet her friends, she realized that she would do anything for his man. He'd been hurt by her mother's attitude to him. Her mother had almost spoiled the plans for tonight. Joshua had been reluctant to allow her to lie, but when she'd pleaded with him, he'd reluctantly consented. He'd wanted to be with her as much as she wanted to be with him.

He came to a sudden stop and turned to her.

He didn't have to say anything. She knew exactly what he wanted. She could see it in his eyes. When his lips touched hers, they were warm but gentle, coaxing her lips apart. When his tongue slipped inside, she shivered, feeling the now familiar heat surge through her body. She felt cold and hot at the same time; a strange feeling, but she basked in the warmth that sped through her body and settled in the juncture between her legs.

The honking of a car horn broke the silence and she pulled away from him, embarrassed by the catcalls of the passengers in the car that had slowed down.

"Come, let's go. It's time we get you by the cinema. Krystal's dad will soon be there."

He reached for her hand and together they walked quickly down Main Street. Krystal was there and Carolyn squeezed Joshua's hand before he moved quickly away. She watched as he disappeared around the corner.

Her body still tingled all over.

Carolyn jumped from her musing. Pain shot up her leg and she looked down to see a duck pecking at her foot. She laughed, shooing it away. Fortunately, it ran off, quacking at its loudest.

Good, she wasn't in the mood for running.

She wondered what her son was doing at this moment. Maybe what he was doing was necessary for him. He needed to discover who he really was and she could not deny him this time of discovery and reflection. Mason had always been very in control of his life, and what she'd told him had created a distance between them that she found scary. Despite the usual self-control he wore like a second skin, his reaction had surprised her. She'd expected anger, but the unexpected silent indifference hurt her.

For several days after his release from hospital, he'd remained in his room, only allowing her in when she'd brought his meals. But he'd hardly eaten anything, preferring to sit by the window watching the world pass by with dull empty eyes.

But like the son she knew, he'd emerged from his room one day, no trace of his anger, a smile on his face, ready to deal with getting on with his life.

She looked toward the lake for the first time since she'd arrived, seeing the smooth rippling of the waves. The waves were so much like her life. Since John's death, she'd tried all she could to purge his constant memory from her life. When she looked back on what had happened when she'd become pregnant at sixteen, she discovered that Joshua had been nothing like she'd expected. Like a silly young child, she'd fallen under the spell of a young boy who knew exactly what to do to get what he wanted. When his guardian had found out, they'd shipped him back to Chicago. Carolyn's mother had been aching to send the police for him, and for the first time she'd defied her mother by refusing to press charges, and for a while had watched each day for him to come up the driveway.

He'd never come.

She'd cried the first time she'd held Mason in her arms. Cried for a man she'd loved and for a father for her child.

Her mother, however, had already taken care of that, and two months later, Carolyn was married to John Sinclair. She'd grown to love the quiet generous teacher of English literature, but a part of her had continued to ache for a love that was never meant to be.

Carolyn never saw Joshua Robert Buchanan again until that day forty years later when she'd opened the paper and his brandy-colored eyes had stared back at her.

Lianne watched as the stranger walked along the beach, seeming oblivious to the activity around him. The daughter of the owner, Melissa, and her two friends, twin girls, stopped and spoke to him for a moment before they rushed off to catch up with a tiny woman sheltered from the sun by a frilly pink parasol. Lianne hadn't seen a parasol in years, but the woman carried it with the gentility of a lady of class.

She'd worked all day taking care of Damien and looked forward to enjoying her evening off. Sheila had agreed to remain within the security of the resort on evenings. Lianne's partner Brent would keep an eye on them since his room was next to the Clarksons' suite. His role as a mystery writer trying to find his muse was perfect. Eventually, he'd strike up a friendship with Sheila, which would allow him to keep even closer to them.

Lianne watched as the man walked along the beach. She'd grown accustomed to the lone figure as he strolled laboriously along the beach each evening for about an hour, before he retreated to a large rocky mass that protruded out to the water's edge and where he sat until the sun disappeared below the horizon. Strange enough, despite his noticeable limp, he seemed alert and fit.

Who was he? Where was he from?

Questions about the stranger remained unanswered.

He intrigued her.

Each evening she came to take a dip in the warm tropical waters, she instinctively searched to find him, experiencing a sense of relief when he was there.

But something bothered her about him. Despite his injury, he seemed alert, on edge, as if expecting the unexpected. A feeling she experienced as naturally as the air she breathed.

Maybe he was a cop.

She was rarely wrong when she had one of her hunches.

She considered following him up the beach, but thought better of the idea. She watched as he sat on the rock and scouted the beach with a casual but careful gaze.

And she had seen him watch her.

Not the casual, careful gaze, but a slow, leisurely

touching of eyes that tingled nerve endings with the promise of things to come.

Maybe he was in the military.

Or maybe he was like her, an agent.

She ached to talk to him, but knew taking her time was important. Yes, they would talk. It was inevitable. She knew it as sure as he did.

The sound of music nearby drew Lianne from her musing. Already the island's local music echoed inside her head. Though it was early September, the songs of last summer's Crop Over Festival could still be heard on the airwaves. Add her knowledge of the songs from the recent Carnival in Trinidad, and she was on her way to becoming a soca expert.

The words of a song she'd become addicted to floated in her head and she closed her eyes, visualizing the music video that showed on television.

The music floated in her head, until she felt the groove. And she danced, right there on the sands with no one watching, or so she thought, until minutes later she opened her eyes and saw *him* watching her.

She blushed, embarrassed because of the spectacle she had made of herself.

"No need to be embarrassed. You dance beautifully. I'd give the singing two thumbs down, but definitely a dancer. You have the spirit of the island in your body."

She smiled, surprised at his easy humor.

"I've only been here for a few weeks but I've already fallen in love with the island and its music. There's something so peaceful and warm about the place and its people."

"I know exactly what you mean. I'd like to see as much of the island as possible, but I'm not too mobile right now."

She heard the anger in his voice and wondered what had caused him to be so angry at the world.

"I had an accident," he responded, as if he'd heard her thoughts, but the information seemed strained from him. She was surprised he didn't offer more.

"I'm sorry." Her voice cracked. For some reason she wished she could take his pain away.

"No need to be. The worst is behind me. At least I'm still alive. I'm not too happy about the limp. Seems like it's a permanent thing, but I'm glad to be alive."

She was about to say sorry again when she stopped. He was definitely not the type to take kindly to empty tokens of empathy.

"You're walking much better than when you arrived, so your leg must be getting stronger. How long ago did you have the…accident?"

"I was in the hospital from the middle of last year until a few weeks ago. When I was discharged I decided to come here. I'd heard so much about the island, I thought this would be a perfect opportunity to visit and deal with my recuperation."

She heard something else in his voice.

Caution?

Wariness?

She wasn't sure.

"So what are you doing on the island?" he asked. "You're the boy's nanny?"

"Yes, I'm his nanny. I've only been working for the family for a year now." The lie slipped from her with ease.

"Nanny? You don't look like anyone's nanny I know."

"I've been told that so often, it's lost its originality. I keep wondering what a nanny's supposed to look like."

"Mary Poppins. Though I must confess I'm partial to Fran Dresher. I wished she were my nanny."

"I've always wanted to work with children. I was a teacher, but when the opportunity came to work for Mrs. Clarkson, I couldn't refuse. The money was too good to be true.

"And the opportunity to travel was also a plus," Lianne said with the greatest of ease.

"Well, you seem to enjoy your job."

"Yes, I do. I won't have missed being on this lovely island. And I love kids. Damien's a sweetheart."

"He does seem a bit quiet. I haven't seen him playing with the other kids staying here," Mason observed.

"I know, but he's a bit shy. I'm sure he'll eventually open up to the other kids in time."

"Well, it's been great chatting with you, but I have to do my thirty minutes of walking before I retire for the night. I haven't had the company of a beautiful woman recently. You enjoy the rest of your night."

He nodded and turned away. Lianne followed his slow movements along the sand. Reluctantly, she turned and was heading in the direction of the resort when she heard his voice asking her to wait.

"You didn't tell me your name. I'm Mason Sinclair."

"Lianne Thomas."

"Nice to meet you, Lianne," he responded, a warm smile touching his lips. "So, how'd you like to walk with me on evenings? I'd love the company and it would give me some motivation."

She laughed. She liked his sense of humor. "I'm not sure if that's a good idea," she replied. "I may only tire you out now your leg is hurt," she teased. "But if you really want the company."

"Oh, I do and I'm definitely up to the challenge. I've been a bit too antisocial since I arrived on the island. I can't think of a better way to spend my evenings than with a beautiful woman."

"Then, I'll like to come, but let me talk to my employer first. I'm sure she won't mind, since she likes to spend the evenings alone with Damien."

"Good, I'd look for you tomorrow. If you're here we'll walk."

With that he turned and continued down the beach.

For a long time she watched him, her brow creased with curiosity.

Mason Sinclair was an interesting man. She'd felt the slam of attraction the first time she'd looked into his eyes. Despite his frailty, there was something strong about the way he carried himself. She wanted to get to know more about Mason. He intrigued her. But she was not sure if she could afford to jeopardize the operation.

No, she did not intend to fall for him, but getting to know him may not be a bad thing.

She only hoped she didn't lose her heart in the process.

During the night Mason awoke to the sound of the rain falling outside. The sound was not harsh but a comforting pitter-patter that was more like the music of the steel pan that played at nights in the resort's dining room. For a while he lay staring at the ceiling. He watched as persistent drops drummed on the windowpanes as if wanting to come into the comfort of his room. He'd grown accustomed to the occasional interrupted nights. Some nights he'd wake to the shattering sound of gunshots. On others, it'd be to the piercing gaze of whiskey-colored eyes taunting him with their familiarity.

So much had happened in his life in the past few months he was beginning to wonder if he was the target of some divine punishment.

From Sam's death, a string of events had hurled him into a stranger's life. He did not feel as if it were his life anymore. He felt like an omniscient observer in the life of a man he didn't really know.

His partner's death, the death of his father, the trip to Barbados, each of the events in his life had combined to confuse him. He did know, however, that he would not return to the Bureau.

For some reason the wave of unhappiness he'd experienced while in hospital no longer weighed heavily on his chest like an anchor.

Today, for the first time, he saw a glimmer of hope and felt the lightness of laughter touch him. His brother's daughter had captured his heart. She was a delightful child and already he'd fallen for her. He wanted to know his niece and the man who'd taken this tiny little girl and called her his own.

His brother must be a very special man.

Just this evening, Mason had seen Taurean on the beach with Melissa, their laughter loud and infectious, and he'd ached to join them, experiencing an overwhelming desire to tell Taurean the truth.

But he knew the time was not right. Maybe Taurean would be able to handle it, but right now he couldn't. Mason needed time to come to grips with the changes in his life before he allowed other people in. For some reason, he knew Taurean would not reject him and he drew comfort from that knowledge.

Tomorrow, he would call his mother and tell her about the island and his brother and niece and the talented woman Taurean called his wife. Mason's call to his mother was long overdue. And she was persistent. Her number had registered on his cell phone more times than he'd thought possible.

And the woman, Bertha, was a riot. He wondered about her role in their life. Was she Alana's family? Was she his aunt? Was she really Melissa's aunt? All these questions tossed themselves around in his head.

He took his cell phone from his pocket and dialed his mother's number. No answer; the answering machine cut in and he left a message in hope she'd call back.

He instinctively dialed a number he hadn't called in days.

"Hello." Clair's gentle voice almost caused him to lose control. Immediately he felt the sting of tears. Talking to her always enforced the reality of

Sam's death. He could not breathe. He wasn't even sure what to say to her.

"Hello, hello, who is it? I can't hear you well."

"Clair, it's Mason."

"Mason, there's a bit too much static on the phone line. I can barely hear you. How are you doing?" she asked.

"I should be the one asking you that question," he responded, despite the tightness in his chest.

There was silence for a moment.

"I'm doing fine, Mason. Life is slowly returning to normal. I still miss Sam so much, but I have to think about the kids." He could hear the pain in her voice, but she sounded better, much better than the last time he'd seen her.

"I'm glad you're learning to live again. Sam would have wanted that. He would have wanted you to put the kids first."

"Yes, thinking about the good times we had and our beautiful children makes living and surviving important."

"Yes, that's what I'm trying to do. Remembering the crazy stuff we did together. I'm just glad I was a part of his life."

"Mason, do you feel that it'll ever stop hurting, that we'll ever stop missing him?"

"I think we'll always remember him, but the hurt will go away. I know it may not seem like that now, but I felt the same way with Dad. And now I just remember him at odd times. But he's always there in my heart."

There was silence.

"So, you're going to let me talk to the girls."

"Of course, I couldn't let Ashley and Kim know you called and I didn't let them speak to you."

He heard her voice shout for the girls and then there was squealing and the loud thunder of stampeding feet.

He spent the next few minutes talking with his two favorite girls and then asked to speak to their mother again.

"Clair, I have to go, but I'll call you again soon. I'm here on the island of Barbados for the next few weeks, but as soon as I'm back in the U.S. I'll come see you and the girls."

"Thanks for calling, Mason. We love you. Oh, and your mother stopped by a few times. We even did lunch."

"That's good. She did tell me she would call. You have a good night, and I'll call soon."

"Bye, Mason."

He heard the gentle click of the phone.

All of a sudden something felt really good inside. Clair and the girls had a habit of making him feel good about himself and life.

Maybe life wouldn't be so bad after all.

Chapter 4

A few days passed before Mason saw Lianne again. He watched as she and the little boy strolled toward the play area just beyond the tennis courts on the left of the resort.

Two nights ago, he'd awoken to excruciating pain as his leg had cramped with spasm after spasm. By morning, he'd had no choice but to go to the doctor. The resort's nurse has recommended a local physician and made arrangements for the resort's driver to take him. Of course, the doctor had informed him that he needed to take things easy and to moderate his walking and exercise, limiting it to once per day.

He'd returned to the resort lightly drowsy from the medication and as soon as he'd reached his room had fallen into a deep sleep. He had remained in bed for the next two days, only calling room service when he'd woken and was hungry enough to eat.

This morning for the first time, he'd been able to move his leg without the soreness he'd grown accustomed to and had felt like stirring. Now, the pain was an annoying throb, but nothing he could not handle.

With awareness came the desire to get out of the confines of his room, but he knew he'd have to take things easy. He would stay upstairs for the rest of the day, watch television, read a book and take a short stroll in the evening. If his leg was feeling any better, he'd eat in the main restaurant. He needed to get out of his room, needed to see some human faces. Ironic for a man who'd preferred being antisocial from his first days at the resort.

He'd go to dinner in the restaurant and maybe he'd see Lianne. She'd been on his mind during his confinement, coming to him in the still of the night. Confession, they say, is good for the soul, and if he had to confess about the number of times he'd made love to the nanny in his dreams, he'd be at confession for hours.

He struggled from the window, his legs feeling

a bit weak, but he took his time, not wanting to irritate anything.

He moved toward the bathroom, needing to take a shower. No, he'd take a bath, to help soak the aches away.

In the bathroom, he saw his reflection in the mirror. He didn't quite like what he saw, but the days in bed had not made things worse. He remembered right after he'd come out of hospital, he'd been shocked at what he'd seen in the mirror. A pale reflection of what he'd seen for years. Once strong and muscular, the image he saw was slim and gaunt, with bones protruding where he'd never seen them before. But since his arrival on the island, he'd begun to fill out again, his arms regaining the tone and his abs hinting at the former six-pack. He would get back to work on that as soon as he could, but this time, he'd take his time and not push himself to the point of exhaustion.

He continued to stare at himself, and then smiled. At least one part of him hadn't got small. To say he was not proud of what God had blessed him with would be a lie. Since his teens, he'd basked in the glory of knowing that women loved him, and when most saw him naked for the first time, they either licked their lips or claimed to have a headache. But all left with a slightly bemused look of contentment on their faces.

He'd always loved women. From the time he'd discovered the joys of sex, he'd indulged for all it was worth. Despite his constant traveling on the job, there'd never been a shortage of women in his bed or *on their knees*.

He remembered when he'd lost his virginity. He'd just turned eighteen, and now, on reflection, that had been late in his life. A friend of his mother, the woman was twice his age, but she'd sniffed at him from the time he'd turned sixteen and had started to fill out.

When she'd seen him naked for the first time, she'd licked her lips and introduced him to the pleasure that came with oral sex.

Then he'd moved into the big league. She'd been amazed that he was a virgin. The first time, he'd ridden her so hard, she'd called him a liar because he'd claimed to be a virgin.

He moved from the mirror, stepped into the shower, and turned the faucet on. He'd leave the bath for another time. A shower would be quicker and he was hungry.

Cool water jolted him, but it was just how he wanted it.

He closed his eyes, but the image that came to him was not the one he'd just been thinking about. Lianne refused to leave his head. She was a distraction and continued to be part of his ongoing discussion with himself and the things that occupied his chamber of thoughts.

He turned the faucets off, grabbed the towel and slowly dried his skin. His body tingled, every nerve sensitive to his touch. Again, he glanced at his body in the mirror, not seeing what was there but recognizing that he was a very sensual man, with needs that at one time had almost consumed him.

Now, he had more control, but Lianne had somehow ingrained herself on his mind. His body stirred again, the heat washing his body with its boldness. He glanced at his arousal, amazed at the power of his manhood, a power he'd learned to control and discipline from an early age.

He put his hand on his chest, feeling the firmness of his body and wishing the hands on him were hers. He sucked his breath in knowing that he had to stop.

He stopped.

He entered the shower again and turned the water on.

He needed to have another shower. Maybe this time, the cold water would do the trick.

Lianne wondered where he was—the man who continued to dominate her every waking moment. She hadn't seen him for a few days and wondered if he'd left the island.

She perused the restaurant, hoping that he'd appear sometime soon. The owner of the resort entered the room, stopping at several of the tables, before he moved to the head table.

She never ceased to be amazed at the uncanny resemblance of Mason to Mr. Buchanan. Each time she saw the two of them near to each other, the similarities became more obvious. Nothing that the average eye would see, but she knew there was something there. Somebody's father had been naughty.

At the odd moment she'd happened to be in close proximity to the two, she'd also noticed that Mason would look at Mr. Buchanan with an odd expression.

There was definitely something there.

When the waitress came to her table, she ordered a simple meal of local flying fish and cou-cou, a wonderful dish she had ordered before and absolutely loved. She'd even searched on the Internet for a recipe but she wasn't sure she could do justice to the unique national dish.

She sat back intending to enjoy the piña colada while she waited for her meal.

Suddenly the hairs behind her neck tingled with the now familiar prick of awareness. She did not have to look around to see who it was. She heard the awkward beat of his footsteps punctuated by the solid staccato of his cane.

The footsteps grew louder and stopped behind her chair.

She looked up. Liquid amber eyes glanced down, an appealing twinkle, quickening the rate of her heartbeat.

"Do you mind if I sit here? All the tables are taken."

She glanced around, noticing several empty tables.

"Okay, I lied, but sitting in the company of a beautiful black woman beats sitting on my own."

Her heart accelerated another notch, but she calmly responded. "Of course you can. I wouldn't mind the company of a handsome black man."

He laughed, lowering himself into the chair opposite. "Touché. I deserve that—but I only speak the truth. You are beautiful."

For a few moments there was an awkward silence, each aware of the intense attraction, but neither knowing what to say.

She broke the silence. "So what are you eating? I'm trying the cou-cou and flying fish. Have you tried it yet?"

"Yes, and I think I'll have the same. It's not my favorite Bajan dish, but I love the flying fish especially if it's fried with those wonderful seasonings the chef here uses."

The waitress interrupted the conversation to take his order and Lianne watched as he charmed the young woman with that infectious smile.

As the girl walked away, Mason turned to Lianne. "So how are you enjoying your stay on the island?" he asked.

"I'm having a great time. I love it here. I never cease to be amazed at the island's beauty. I've heard so much about the Caribbean, but never knew they were so beautiful."

"I know what you mean. I'm looking forward to going into the water, but I can't yet." He noticed her look. "My leg's still not totally healed."

"I don't mean to pry, but what happened?"

"I was shot on duty."

"You're a cop?"

"No, I'm an FBI agent. I've been on medical leave. Lost my partner in the shooting."

"I'm sorry to hear. Losing someone special is not easy."

"Yes, Sam was pretty special. He was my partner for ten years. It's his wife, Clair, and their two kids I'm more concerned about. It's not been easy for them. As least they don't have to worry about finances."

"Two of you must have been really close."

"Yeah, he was like the brother I always wanted. It's not easy being an only child." He paused as if he realized he'd said too much about himself. "But enough about me. What's a lovely woman like you doing being a nanny?"

Trying to remain calm, Lianne launched into the rehearsed speech she'd planned.

"I'm not even sure what made me want to be a nanny. I was an only child and remember being very lonely. One of the kids in my neighborhood had a nanny who I thought was the nicest person. Maybe I feel an empathy with children with no brothers or sisters and know the importance of having someone close. I got tired of being a teacher, so being a nanny just seemed the natural thing to do."

"So you've been doing this for…"

The waitress interrupted again, carrying the two meals perched skillfully on one hand. Quickly completing her task, she told them to enjoy their meal and call for her if they needed anything.

Without hesitation they dug into the meal with gusto, both preferring to savor the exotic dish.

Much later, contented, Lianne leaned back against the chair and found Mason's eyes on her. She blushed, feeling awkward that he'd been watching her eating.

"I love to see a woman who can enjoy her food. I get so annoyed when I take a woman out and all she does is pick at the food all night like a bird on a diet."

She laughed. "Oh, I'd always had a hearty appetite. It's all the exercising I do that keeps me at this size. I've always been very fit. And having a mother that loves to cook didn't help much while I was growing."

He joined her in laughter, enjoying the sound of her husky voice.

"I'm a lot like you. I'm an only child. It's always been my mother—" he hesitated "—my father and me. When I was young I always wished for a brother or a sister." Something in his voice made her look at him closely. He almost seemed sad.

Curiosity got the best of her and she was about to ask the question on her mind when he jumped to his feet abruptly, knocking his cane to the floor. He fumbled for it before he straightened.

"I have to go," was all he said. He took his wallet from his back pocket and placed several bills on the table. "Dinner is on me."

And then he was gone.

She watched in amazement as he stumbled away. What had she done wrong? What had she said to cause such an unexpected reaction? She was actually beginning to enjoy his company. She searched in her mind, trying to recall part of the conversation.

Was it his father?

Or mother?

She couldn't think clearly. The unexpected disappointment at his departure hung like a gray cloud above her. She'd go find Damien and Sheila. They would be in the activities room for kids. A local storyteller was scheduled to entertain the kids one evening each week but, since she'd been before, she wanted to do something different.

Or maybe she'd just go back to her room and spend the rest of the night watching television.

She beckoned to the waitress, took the bill and placed the money Mason had left on the table, leaving a generous tip.

Lianne left the room, the feeling of euphoria gone. Mason Sinclair did something to her. No man in recent years had stirred her in the way he did. He left her feeling breathless, light-headed and flustered at the same time. Like a teenager falling in love for the first time.

And she was definitely no teenager.

Was she falling in love?

Definitely not!

To her, love was not a part of the equation of her life. She'd had relationships, but she refused to allow herself to come under any man's control again. The relationship with one of her colleagues in her mid-twenties had only proved that remaining in control of one's own existence made life a lot easier.

No, she definitely had no intentions of falling in love.

* * *

Mason didn't realize how far he'd walked until he turned around and saw the resort far in the distance. He glanced at his watch, the dark night crystal illuminating the Roman numerals.

His eyes were slowly adjusting to the darkness, the shadows on the water taking the shape of fishing boats. He moved toward a small fishing boat that had seen better days and appeared no longer seaworthy. He could feel the throbbing in his leg slowly building and chided himself for coming so far.

What had just gone wrong? He couldn't understand why he'd raced out of the restaurant. Lianne has a strange effect on him. Women had always come to him easily, and there had been many, but none had ever caused him to think. Yes, that was it! The others had all been about sex and mutual gratification. With Lianne, it was different. She made him dream of babies and happily-ever-after….

No, he was not going to let that happen. He needed to think about his future. A woman at this time would only complicate his already disheveled life.

He needed to call his mother. By now, she'd be getting worried, and he wanted to reassure her that all was going well.

He needed to talk to someone. Sam would be the perfect one to…

Sam.

He kept forgetting. Sam was no longer around.

The nightmares still came. Not as frequent as before, but every few nights he was sure to wake after feeling the white pain of a bullet entering his body.

And the blood.

There was always so much blood.

Ironically, that day had started with the promise of sunshine…. By nighttime, his life had changed….

Mason honked on the horn and watched as his partner hustled from the house. He'd dropped Sam off just under three hours ago, but before he could comfortably settle into dreamworld, the phone had rung, bringing him back to the reality of his demanding job.

But the call could not be ignored. A break in a case they'd been working on for the past few months finally promised an ending to hours of work. The serial killer, the Poet, would finally be in custody.

In the past two weeks, they'd come closest to discovering the identity of the man. A few days ago, they'd finally put things together and all fingers pointed to local playboy Justin Cunningham.

Mason watched as Sam kissed his wife and the baby in her arms. Ashley and Kim would be at school, but the simple image of the domestic life was endearing and sweet.

At that time, he ached like all the other mornings when he'd seen Sam kiss Clair goodbye. Mason watched as Sam released the baby to his mother and walked quickly to the car.

Mason waved at Clair and she responded, a smile of concern on her face. Though Clair supported Sam in all that he did, there were moments when Mason saw the look of despair whenever they went out on a mission and Sam was away from her for days and sometimes weeks. He couldn't be Sam. He definitely did not want to leave his wife in that state of mind.

While the car sped down the highway, Mason took the opportunity to talk to Sam.

"Something wrong with Clair? She doesn't look too happy."

At first, he did not respond, instead beginning to flick through the channels.

"She wants me to leave the agency. She's pregnant again and says she can't go through this one alone again. I told her I'd take leave, but she doesn't want that. She says she can't live like this anymore. Always wondering if I'd come home or not."

"So what are you going to do?"

"I don't know. I've thought of it for the past few weeks and I'm still not sure. I want to be with her, but I still love my job, too." Mason could hear the despair in his voice. "It's not fair when women do this craziness to us. Why are we the ones to always compromise?"

"Sam, you can't look at it that way. I'm sure that Clair would have to be dealing with a lot to ask you to do this."

"But I can't understand why I can't have both. The likelihood that I'll get killed is as likely as my getting knocked down on the road."

"True, but you need to put yourself in her position. Would you want to be pregnant and have your husband away most of the time and with a dangerous job to boot?"

"I thought you were my partner."

"Yes, I am, but I can still see things from her position."

Sam was silent as if internalizing what Mason had said.

By this time they'd reached the outskirts of the city and driven into an area they both frequented. The mood had passed and they were discussing the evidence from another case they were working.

Jacksonville was known for its many vices. Drugs, prostitution and gambling were part of the lifestyle of the residents. Mason and Sam avoided the area as much as possible, but the lead to Cunningham was one they could not ignore.

Mason parked the car in front of the four-story

apartment building that had seen better days. But it was not out of place, since the buildings on each block were replicas of each other.

Jumping from the old Ford they'd driven for five years, Mason followed Sam to the entrance of the apartment building where Cunningham had been seen entering several hours ago. Seemed his new girl lived there.

Fortunately, two women were exiting the building, so there was no need for anyone to let them in.

Sam pressed the elevator when they reached it, but no such luck. It was not working.

They moved to the stairs, Sam racing ahead, taking the stairs two at a time.

When Mason heard the first gunshot, a sharp coldness raced up his body. Turning the corner, he lost his footing as Sam stumbled back on him, his shirt covered in blood.

As Mason reached for his gun, he heard the telltale click of a trigger before he felt the jolt of a bullet enter his leg. Excruciating pain almost felled him, but not before he fired his own gun, his fingers pulling the trigger as bullet after bullet entered the man standing above him.

The last thing he remembered was the look on the man's face as he stood erect and then crashed to the landing, his body rolling with the momentum from the stairs.

Hours later when Mason woke up groggy and a bit disoriented, Clair sat by his bed. Her eyes were closed. She must have heard him stir, and her eyes slowly opened.

Mason saw the moisture in her eyes and knew immediately what had happened. He felt the sting of tears.

"I'm sorry," he told her, his arms outstretched. "I'm so sorry."

She stood slowly and then raced to his arms and he continued to hold her as she cried for the man that he loved like a brother....

The barking drew him from that painful place where he hated to go. He turned toward the noise and saw his dog, the dog he called Beach, going round and round in circles as he tried to catch his tail.

Eventually, the barking stopped and Beach plopped to the ground, his tongue hanging out the side, saliva dripping on the sand.

His eyes focused on Mason, and then seemed to soften. On his stomach, he crawled closer, his eyes not losing the stare, until he lay just in front of Mason.

Mason extended his hand and Beach eyed it coyly. Then his tongue flicked and tasted Mason's hand.

"Come, my brave warrior," Mason said. "Come, let's be friends."

With no hesitation, the dog stood and rested his head on Mason's lap, closing his eyes. Mason petted his head, enjoying the feel of the texture of his fur.

For now, thoughts of Sam and Clair and Lianne were forgotten. Instead the complete trust of a lonely dog left him overwhelmed.

Lianne slipped from the back entrance of the resort. Mrs. Clarkson and Damien had long gone to bed and she needed to meet with Monroe or Smart to get an update. It was their weekly plan, so she'd go to the bar on the beach and he'd join her there, pretending to strike up a conversation with her.

The beach was quiet; only the dimmed lights allowed passage to the tiny but popular bar. A voice screeched the lyrics of Whitney Houston's "All the Man that I Need."

Lord, she should turn back, but that was what karaoke was all about. Just enjoying yourself.

She slipped into a solitary chair at the back of the bar and watched all that was going on as she waited. The woman had finished her painful off-key rendition of Whitney's "All the Man that I Need," and had been replaced by a slightly overweight man who was bent on enjoying himself. He broke into a hilarious and energetic version of Lionel Richie's "All Night Long," and soon several of the other guests were standing, dancing and joining him on the chorus.

She glanced at her watch wondering if either Smart or Monroe would make the contact. In the time before their arrival on the island, she and Brent had gotten to know the two agents and admired their quick minds. An easy rapport had sprung up between them. She enjoyed working with them and had grown fond of the two in record time. They'd done all in their power to make sure she'd been ready for her position as nanny in a few days.

She glanced at her watch again. If one of them didn't arrive in the next few minutes, she'd leave. She didn't want to appear too obvious in her wait for someone.

As if he'd heard her, Agent Smart sat in the empty chair at her table and immediately she switched into agent mode.

"So how's it going, Thomas? Enjoying the island life?"

"Sure, haven't enjoyed karaoke for a long time. I've forgotten how much fun it could be. So is there anything interesting to report?"

"Nothing much has changed. Jury selection is over, and the trial is underway. From all sources, there're no strange activities."

"That's good to know."

"So how are Mrs. Clarkson and her son doing?"

"The boy seems to be doing fine. He loves the beach so we've been going there most days, but I'm sure you've noticed. We plan to go to several of the places of interest—the museum, Harrison's Cave. The resort plans several tours each week. Mrs. Clarkson…I'm not too sure about. She's not talking or saying much. She only says anything to me when it's necessary. I know she must be worried."

"Well, you just have to continue reassuring her that we're in control of everything. She has nothing to be afraid of."

"I'm doing that. In the meantime, I want you to do something for me. Run a check on a Mason Sinclair. He says he's a special agent on leave. Shot in the line of duty."

"Think he may be someone we need to check on?" he asked.

"Doesn't seem so, but I just want to be sure. I don't want to make any mistakes I'll regret later."

"Okay, will do. I'll report back to you at the scheduled time next week. This karaoke session is a perfect time to meet. Maybe you should go do a song."

"Yes, sure," she responded, her voice light with sarcasm.

She turned to watch the couple who'd taken the stage and heard the intro of one of her favorite songs, "You Don't Bring Me Flowers." She hoped they didn't slaughter it.

Five minutes later, she was clapping and whistling with the other guests and locals as the couple left the stage.

She felt the familiar prickle at her neck and turned around.

Mason.

His stare was deep and intense, and their gazes met halfway.

He smiled at her and then turned and walked away.

Had he seen her talking to Smart? She hoped not. For a moment she lost her composure. She'd not expected anyone to notice her, since at the karaoke sessions, people tended to focus on what was going on onstage.

Oh, she needn't worry. He'd probably assume that someone at the hotel had been trying to hit on her.

But he was an agent, wasn't he?

Maybe the meeting in a public area was not such a good idea after all.

In future she had to be even more careful.

Carolyn observed the ducks as they swam and bobbed on the park's lake. For some reason, and despite her initial run-in with them, she found their interaction with each other quite fascinating. She'd come here for the second time this week, and as always she felt a sense of calm as she watched one of God's least elegant creatures.

The day could only be called perfect with its

white fluffy clouds and brilliant sunshine. Yes, it was hot, but the gentle breeze provided the coolness to temper the heat.

She felt like singing and dancing, all the things she'd done as a child, but the man who sat just a few benches away forced her to remain the lady she'd worked so hard to cultivate.

Without warning, a high gust whipped across the park, taking the colorful scarf she'd taken from her hair and placed around her neck. She raced after it, thinking of the spectacle she must be making of herself, but determined to catch the scarf before it ended in the lake.

Carolyn came to a halt when the man stood and gallantly caught the scarf in his hand. As he straightened, he turned in her direction and she saw his face for the first time.

He was fine.

Since John's death, she'd enjoyed the company of several men—enjoyed their beds—but there was something about this black Adonis that caused her heart to thump painfully against her chest. She gasped for air, realizing that she held her breath.

He was definitely fine.

Feeling a bit embarrassed at her display, though she knew he could not be aware of her reaction, she counted to ten, regaining her poise, and walked with as much elegance as she could muster toward her scarf rescuer.

When she reached him, she tittered daintily. *What was wrong with her?*

"Thank you. I don't know what I would have done if it had flown into the water. And it's my favorite scarf."

"For a woman as beautiful as you, I'd have dived into the water and rescued it."

"Aren't *you* the perfect gentleman?"

And then she really looked at him for the first time.

He was fine…and young. At least younger than her forty years. Okay, fifty-six, but who was counting? He had to be in his mid-forties, just a bit older that Mason.

Damn, he was fine.

God, she was beginning to sound like a record that had stuck.

"I've never been called a gentleman before. But it does feel good to know that someone thinks so. Even if the fact that you're a stranger means you really don't know me."

"So does that mean I'm wrong and you're some kind of mass murderer?"

"No, nothing as notorious as that. I'm a professor at the university."

"I'm Carolyn Sinclair, Mr. Professor. It's a pleasure to meet you." She stressed the word *pleasure*.

"And I'm Professor Garth Wade. But I'd prefer if we continue this conversation on the bench over there. If you don't mind?"

She didn't mind, so she followed him.

The perfect gentleman, he waited until she sat before lowering himself next to her.

"Your scarf?" Nice, strong hands. She loved a man with strong hands.

"Oh, thank you. Wouldn't want to forget it. I'd have to come by your home and pick it up."

"So I'm having an effect on you?" His voice was deep and husky with emotion.

"Are you flirting with me? I'm a bit too old for you."

"Age doesn't matter when it comes to attraction…and love. But we'll deal with that issue later. For now, let's just get to know each other."

"Maybe that's not such a good idea."

"What's not a good idea? Two strangers meeting for the first time and getting to know each other?"

"You know what I mean."

"What do you mean?" he asked.

"Yes, stranger…this flirtation…our ages. You don't know anything about me. I don't know anything about you."

"So let's rectify the problem. Let's do dinner. At a neutral place. I'll give you my department head's number. I'm sure she would act as a reference." He paused for a moment. "I really want to get to know you."

"Let me think about it. I have some friends that work at the university." She didn't want to tell him she knew the dean and several members of the board.

"Okay, here's my card. Call me anytime. I wish I could stay a bit longer, but I have a class at four o'clock." He reached for her hand. "I hope you'll call."

She didn't know what to say. All she felt was the warmth of his hand and the racing of her heartbeat. With a final smile, he turned and walked away.

Yes, he was fine.

Carolyn sat there for the rest of the afternoon, enjoying the latest romance from her favorite author. Though she loved romance novels, she'd always believed they stretched the boundaries of reality. Maybe she was wrong. What had just happened to her was out of a romance novel. Her marriage to John had been a marriage of convenience and over the years she'd grown to love him in a safe, undemanding way. She would never be able to love Garth Wade like that. He would want much, much more. He would want her soul, and she knew that as much as she knew she would want the same thing from him. Already his image was fixed on her mind's eye, vivid and strong.

She knew she'd go out with him. She would have

agreed immediately, but she needed to be sure she was doing the right thing.

She was an icon in the community and she did not want to cause a scandal, but scandal she knew it would be. Oh, she could hear it now. She'd be like Stella wanting to get her groove on. In Europe she could do whatever she wanted without raising an eyebrow. Here in her tiny, narrow-minded hometown, things were totally different.

But she didn't care. Garth Wade was the perfect person to do it with. Hell, she was going to throw caution to the wind and see where this was going.

She was a goner.

But damn, he was fine.

The darkness hid the alley's ugliness, but the man who cautiously entered welcomed the lack of light. He wanted no one to see him. Guilt weighed heavily on his chest but his financial needs demanded that he betray all that he'd worked to achieve for the past ten years. A wave of sadness for what he was about to do caused him to shiver. Coming here had been the final step into corruption and betrayal.

Something rattled to his left and he jumped. He expected the cat that usually appeared at this time in movies to provide a moment of comic relief but none appeared, only the steady footsteps of the one he was to meet.

A tall shadow strolled toward him and stopped.

"Do you have the information?" The voice was flat, husky, void of emotion.

"Yes. You have the money?"

There was laughter. A hollow sound that grated on his ears.

"Greedy aren't we?"

Another wave of guilt, but he did not respond, only groped in his coat pocket and withdrew the envelope that seemed to burn his hand.

He took the bag the man handed him in return and the first glimmer of hope made what he'd done justifiable.

"If the information is not correct, I'll find you," came the voice, and then he was gone, vanished into the darkness.

The man turned, heading quickly in the direction he'd come. He needed to get home to his wife. Watching her come to life again would be worth selling his soul to the devil.

But he knew that tonight he would say a prayer for Sheila Clarkson and her son.

Chapter 5

Mason knew he had to apologize. After chiding himself for the whole day, he knew he had to do the inevitable, but he had not seen Lianne for the day. When he inquired about her, he discovered that she and the family she worked for had gone on one of the fun cruises that the guests of the resort attended weekly. In the meantime, there was nothing to do but wait.

Last night, he'd been surprised to see her at the karaoke session, since he'd never seen her there before. He'd fallen asleep in the late afternoon after taking his medication and had arrived late, but just in time to see the man leave her table.

He wondered who the man was and why he'd been talking to Lianne.

He wasn't totally sure, but there was something familiar about the man. Maybe he'd seen him around the resort. But something felt wrong about what he'd seen. Yes, he'd not seen much, but Lianne had seemed unperturbed by the man's intrusion, so Mason had discounted her not knowing him. For the briefest of moments, she'd appeared slightly unsettled. He could tell that she wondered if he'd seen the man.

He wanted to know more about her, but for what reason, he wasn't sure. Maybe there was something suspicious going on, but why would he want to be involved?

What surprised him was the sharp jolt of jealousy he'd felt when he'd seen the man talking to her. That had never been a problem in the past. He never, ever allowed himself to get emotionally attached to any of the women in his life, however long they were able to hold his interest.

A sharp pain raced up his leg and he chided himself again for his folly. In the early hours of the morning, unable to sleep, he'd tried running on the beach, but had only aggravated his leg. Would he ever learn? The specialist had emphasized that time was important for him to heal properly.

Deep inside he knew he'd never be totally whole again. His decision to leave the agency was the best decision he'd made. With his bum leg, there was definitely no going back. When his leave was officially up, he'd have to let his boss know.

The voice of Usher drew him from his musings. His cell phone. He glanced down at the number.

His mother.

He pressed the talk button and his mother's voice came to him, clear and articulate.

"Mason, this is your mother. How are you doing?"

Damn, did she always have to be so formal? "I'm doing fine, Mother. The island is beautiful. You'd love it here."

"That's good. So are you taking care of that leg? Found a good doctor on the island?"

"Yes, I've found a good doctor. And yes, I've been walking on the beach and healing well. I' not in pain too often now and the leg is getting stronger." He was not being totally honest, but he didn't want her to worry too much. She'd probably board the next plane if she knew he was overworking his leg.

"That's good to know. I worry about you." Her voice was calm, but sincere. "Have you met your brother?"

"Not officially. His name is Taurean and he seems like a good person. He's married and has a stepdaughter. She's a smart little girl. I haven't introduced myself to his wife Alana yet. She's spending some time at a beach house they own finishing a painting for a show she has coming up. She's an artist."

"Alana…Buchanan. Where have I heard that name before? Oh…she's the artist who had that show last year in New York and won all those awards. I'm definitely going to have to come to Barbados and meet her. I was actually planning to purchase one I saw at the show, but they all went so quickly."

"You must let me know what you think. So how are you doing, Mother?"

"I'm fine…I…" she fumbled her words.

"Yes." Mason couldn't remember when he'd ever heard his mother at a loss for words.

"I was wondering if you'd approve if I went on a date."

His first instinct was to burst out laughing, but then the reality of what she'd just asked him took the matter to a more serious level.

His mother was asking permission to go on a date. The woman who had been partying and enjoying the company of several men over the past few years. This must be serious. It wasn't often his mother was in a fluster.

"Mom, there's no need for you to ask me about going on a date. You're my mother…. Not the other way around."

"I mean...your father. Do you think he'd mind?"

"Mom, I'm sure Dad would want you to be happy. Go out and enjoy yourself."

Again she seemed at a loss for words. "Thanks, I just wanted to be sure I was doing the right thing."

"Of course, you're doing the right thing. You're doing what you want."

"Thank you, Mason, for understanding. You take care of yourself now. And don't you overdo it with that leg."

"I won't."

"Goodbye. Love you."

"Love you too, Mom."

The line disconnected and Mason placed the phone in his pocket.

His mother was going on a date. He'd never thought he'd see the day arrive. Strange that she'd called and asked his permission. She'd never introduced him to any of her "friends," so this man had to be special. Mason realized he should have asked her about the man. Who was he? What did he do?

Life was strange. One day your life was perfect. You had the job of your dreams and then a whole string of crazy things happened and you didn't know where your life was heading.

Enough of those crazy things had happened to him in the last year.

Sam's death, his leg, his mother's revelation, and now all that was happening to him on the island.

All he hoped was that when the waves settled he'd have some semblance of a life.

Lianne watched as Sheila and Damien danced to the rhythm of the sweet calypso music. The pirate cruise on the *Jolly Roger* had turned out to be as exciting as she'd expected. Several of the resort's guests had been before and raved about the fun time they'd had. They'd left the resort around ten this morning to reach the Bridgetown Harbor where the authentic schooner lay docked. Not a cruise ship in the typical sense of the word, but a ship, with no cabins, and just lots and lots of space to party.

Locals and tourist mingled, jumped, waved and gyrated to the pulsating, pounding rhythm of the most recent calypso tunes. Crop Over, the island national cultural festival had just passed and, despite the ending of the official time of revelry, the popular songs of the festival rose from the large speakers dotted at strategic locations on the ship.

The schooner provided everything for the tourist looking for adventure. From the crew dressed in authentic pirates' costume to "walking the plank," each of the activities provided entertainment and excitement for the four-hour cruise.

Like the other adults onboard, Lianne had

sampled the notorious pirate rum punch and dived into the clear waters when the schooner had anchored off the west coast near Holetown.

Originally called Jamestown after King James I, the town's significance lay in its settlement by the English, who landed in 1625.

Now, Lianne reclined on one of the many lounge chairs that lined the upper deck, absorbing the golden sunshine and watching the huge red sails billowing in the wind and the skull-and-crossbones flag reminiscent of the pirate ships that had infested the waters of the Caribbean in the past.

In the midst of all the excitement, Lianne wondered what Mason was doing. She should have invited him to come with them, but unsure about his response, she'd decided against it. She was still puzzled by his behavior the other night.

Lianne watched as Sheila Clarkson made her way toward her and slipped into the lounge chair next to hers. Sheila appeared a bit uncomfortable. Despite the few weeks they'd been employee and employer, Sheila had not said much to her. Lianne hoped this was about to change. She waited for her to speak.

"Do you know how my husband is doing? I've wanted to ask before, but Damien is always around."

"He's doing fine. I spoke to my contact on the island last night. There's been nothing to indicate we have anything to worry about…yet." She wanted to put the woman's mind at rest, but she didn't want to fool her that Cordoni would do nothing. "We're doing everything we can to keep him safe."

"I know that. I'm scared, but there was never a doubt in my mind that Jason would do the right thing. My husband is a noble, honest man. Yes, there were doubts, but I knew he couldn't live with himself if he didn't do what his heart knew was right."

"You're lucky to have found someone so special. There are very few men like him."

"I know…and you're looking for that kind of person, too. I can see your loneliness."

Lianne looked Sheila directly in her eyes, seeing a woman more that ten years younger than she was but yet there was a maturity in her eyes that hinted at the life she'd lived.

"Your husband is a lucky man too. He has a wife who loves him and an adorable son. It must have been a hard decision for him to make."

"Yes, it was. Hard to let me know that he had to do this. Putting our lives in danger was one of the hardest decisions he has ever made. He made sure that we were taken care of before he made the decision to testify. But let's talk no more of this. We're here to enjoy ourselves. Damien's enjoying himself with the other kids. Let's talk about clothes, movies, soap operas, anything that a woman would talk about."

At Lianne's snort of disgust, Sheila laughed, a husky, deep sound that belied the seriousness on her face.

"I'm only kidding. I know your job does not allow you those feminine vices. Tell me about your job. What made you want to be an agent?"

No one had ever asked her that question. At least no one had asked her that question and received an honest answer.

"It was my best friend. When I was in high school, she was murdered because she happened to be in the wrong place."

"I'm sorry."

"It was a long time ago. She was kidnapped when a group of men tried to rob a bank. They took her for two weeks before we found her body. I vowed then that I would do all I could to stop people who hurt innocent people."

"Your parents must be proud of you."

"At first they weren't, but when my father realized why I wanted to be an agent, he was as supportive as possible. My mother still doesn't understand why I'm doing what I do. She accepted that she can't change it, but always says she wanted so much more for me."

"It must not be easy doing what you do."

"No, it's not easy. I hate the killing, but there's nothing like seeing the faces of those whose loved ones we've saved. It doesn't happen as often as it should, but it makes all that I do worth it."

"You're like my husband. Noble and brave."

Lianne didn't know what to say.

"Maybe…I've never seen myself in that light."

"Oh, I do…and so does Damien. He believes you're better that any super hero. He knows you're definitely not Mary Poppins."

Lianne's laughter joined Sheila's.

"I hope I can live up to his expectations. You have an adorable and smart boy."

"He's like his father. When he overheard his father and I discussing the case, he came to us and told us not to worry, that we needed to do the right thing and that God would take care of us."

"He's a brave boy."

As if he'd heard them talking about him, Damien appeared at the top of the stairway and glanced around trying to find them.

"Mum, Mum, come quickly. They want us to walk the gangplank again. Can I? Can I?"

"Lianne, come let's go watch. He won't stop asking unless I let him go. I may just get the courage to do it, too." She leaned over and whispered in Lianne's ear. "Thanks for listening."

* * *

Carolyn had been staring at the phone for the past three hours, knowing that she would inevitably make that phone call, but each time she picked it up, another creative excuse for why she shouldn't get involved with Garth Wade was added to her already long list of excuses.

Several days had passed since meeting him and she'd done exactly what she'd planned. She'd called the dean of Garth's faculty and made a discreet inquiry. William, the dean, had not asked any questions but she'd heard the curiosity in his voice.

So what had she learned about him?

Forty-six, published, with several books on Caribbean literature, widowed, loved jazz and old black-and-white movies.

Interesting…

She could go with the jazz and the old black-and-white movies.

Okay, she knew that she had to do it or lose her cool again….

She picked up the phone again and dialed the number she'd long memorized.

Garth picked it up on the second ring.

"Hello, Carolyn." She heard the hint of laughter in his voice before he continued. "Wondered how long it would take you to find the courage to call."

"I just hate this caller-ID feature that everyone

seems to have these days. It means that if I'd chick-
ened out, you'd have been there dying of laughter.
You'd know I called and put down."

"Okay, Carolyn, I'm sorry, I didn't mean to
laugh at you. I'm glad you called. Forgive me." His
voice was calm, sincere.

"Okay, sorry I'm a bit testy. I'm not sure I
know how to handle this…" She wasn't sure what
to call it.

"Friendship," he offered.

"Yes. Friendship."

"As I say, I'm glad you called. I hoped you'd call
earlier. Now, I can finally stop running to the phone
each time it rings. I've been staying in at night in
hope that you called."

"You didn't have to do that."

"Yes, I did."

Again, she was at a loss for words.

"I was beginning to think you didn't want to go
out with me."

"No, I just had to do some serious thinking."

"About going on a date with me? Why the fuss?
It'll just be a simple date," he said, trying to sound
flippant.

Sexual tension charged the silence.

"No, that's not true," he said, his voice husky
with emotion. "It won't be just a simple date."

Her first reaction was to deny his claim, but it

would have been silly to deny the intensity of the attraction between them.

"Yes, it definitely won't be just a date. But attraction isn't all to a relationship."

"Don't I know that, but it's a good start."

"It is?"

"Listen, Carolyn. We're two grown adults who are attracted to each other. We're not committing to years of marital bliss. We're just two friends getting to know each other. I don't know where this is going to lead, but let's just give friendship a chance before we make a mountain out of a molehill."

There was a simple truth in what he said.

"Okay, I can live with that," she responded.

"Good. So we're friends?"

"Yes, friends."

"Good. So when can we go on that date you promised me?"

"Me? Promised?" she teased.

"So you don't want to go on a date with me? I'm hurt." She heard the laughter in his voice.

"I didn't say that. Don't put words in my mouth. If you promise to be on your best behavior and get me back home at a respectable time, I'd love to go to dinner with you."

"Of course, I'll be on my best behavior. My momma taught me how to be a gentleman."

"That's left to be seen."

"So how's Saturday for you? You like jazz?"

"Yes, and old black-and-white movies, too?"

"Oh, so you've been checking up on me?"

"Just a bit. William didn't tell any secrets. I just asked him what he thought of you."

"So you know the dean?"

"Yes, we're old friends. My late husband was a professor there, too."

"Sinclair... John Sinclair was your husband? He was my thesis supervisor when I was doing my Master's. Man, when I got assigned to him I was so excited. He was one of the most knowledgeable scholars on Caribbean literature."

"Yes, he was one of the best."

"It was an honor to work with him. He was a good man."

"I know. I was married to him."

"Damn, Carolyn, I'm so sorry. Here I am rattling on about your late husband."

"No need to apologize. I was just teasing. It doesn't hurt anymore when I talk about him. In fact, it feels good when people remember him and acknowledge his contribution to his field. John was passionate about his work. He was a passionate man. I loved him."

"You must have really loved him."

"I did despite the circumstance under which we got married, but I learned to love him. When he died,

I felt as if my life was over. It's only because of Mason that I knew I had to continue living. But, let's not talk about that now. One of these days I'll tell you the story, but for now just let's talk about dinner."

"That's fine. So how about I pick you up Saturday at 7:00 p.m. We'll do dinner and then go to a club which plays the most awesome jazz."

"I look forward to it."

"You enjoy the rest of your night. I have some papers to grade before tomorrow. Sleep well and stay beautiful."

Five minutes after he'd put the phone down, Carolyn still held it to her breasts.

As had become her custom, Lianne sat on the wall looking out to sea. She tried not to focus on the thoughts that flashed through her mind. Lianne wondered if he'd come. She'd not seen Mason take his daily walk in the past few days and wondered if he'd left the island. She still wondered what had caused him to leave the dinner table so abruptly the other night.

The brooding silent man came easily to her mind these days, a fact that she wasn't too pleased about, but one she seemed to have no control over. She saw him in every corridor and around every corner. Yesterday, while shopping in Bridgetown, she thought she'd seen him in Cave Shepherd, the island's largest department store.

As the beach lights flicked on, the shadows of coconut trees that lined the path to the beach disappeared, revealing a couple locked in deep embrace. Standing hastily, they linked hands and disappeared into the darkness.

A smile touched Lianne's lips. She hoped they found a stop that was as private and secluded. Then the unexpected happened—a sharp wanting she'd rather not acknowledge.

She wanted that for herself. Someone to touch and steal kisses with in the shadows of coconut trees.

She closed her eyes, willing the feeling to leave her.

When she opened them, he stood there.

Mason walked slower than usual and immediately she knew that something was wrong. He stopped suddenly, looked around, his gaze resting where she sat.

Her heartbeat quickened as he drew near. When Mason reached her, he stopped, his smile broad and inviting.

"Hi," he greeted.

"Hi," she echoed. "I thought you'd left the island."

"You did? I wouldn't have left without letting you know."

"I was looking forward to our walks on the beach, getting some exercise." His comment warmed her. Her anger no longer made sense. She'd jumped too quickly to a negative conclusion.

"I'm sorry, Lianne. My leg decided I'd over-worked it enough, and cramped up two nights ago. Mr. Buchanan took me to the hospital. I've been there until this morning."

"Oh, are you going to be all right?"

"Yes, I'll be fine. It just feels a bit sore, but the medication has helped. I'm just a bit drowsy, but the doctor says it's nothing to worry about."

"Does that mean no more walking?"

"No, it just means I have to take things easy. I've not been very patient when it comes to my recovery. I hate the inactivity. So, I'm putting myself in your care. You're responsible for making sure I don't exert myself too much."

"Me? Do I get to be your nanny, too?" she teased.

"Sure, if that's what you want to call it."

"Well, since I don't seem to have too much of a choice, we'll begin tomorrow. You'll come swim with Damien and me in the mornings and then we'll walk a bit in the evenings. Does that schedule seem reasonable?"

"That's perfect. I think I'm going to enjoy being under your care."

"Good, and since you're already here, let's take a short stroll down the beach. We won't go too far."

Lianne allowed him to lead the way. Falling comfortably in step with him, they headed away from the resort.

"I'm definitely missing my usual workout in the gym," Lianne said. "Unfortunately, the resort doesn't have one, though Mr. Buchanan says there is an arrangement with a local gym. However, the time is a bit too early for me."

"So you work out? I wondered what was responsible for that exquisite figure."

Lianne blushed. "Just a gym near to my apartment. Nothing fancy like Jenny Craig, but it keeps me fit for…" She paused. She'd almost fouled up and said *the job*, but held herself back.

He glanced at her strangely, but said nothing.

For a while they walked in silence, the only sound the gentle lap of the surf against the shore. Lianne hoped he didn't think too much of her almost slip of the tongue.

Fifteen minutes later, he stopped, his breathing calm and controlled like hers, but they'd noticeably slowed.

"We'll turn back here," he said, "but I need to take a bit of a rest. I usually sit on the rocks over there."

She followed him, allowing him to sit first, and then joined him, sure to sit a reasonable distance from him. Being close to Mason did strange things to her.

.   The silence continued until he said, "How long are you going to be on the island?"

"For another few weeks. I'm not exactly sure, but Sheila's working on a travel book about the island. We have several more places of interest to visit, but she says the island has been good for Damien, so we may stay until she's ready to go."

"A travel writer. Sounds like an interesting job. You get to travel all over the world."

"I enjoy it. We were in England a few weeks ago." The lies slipped from her with the ease of years of practice and experience. Well, it wasn't a complete lie since that's where she'd spent her summer.

"I've done a lot of traveling, but England is one place I've never been to," he said. "I've always been a bit intimidated by the primness of the English."

"Oh, England is a beautiful place but there's just something about the lushness of the tropics that I love. I'd love to settle here on the island one day."

"I know what you mean."

There was a barking in the distance.

"That's Beach."

"Beach?"

"A stray dog that roams the beach. He doesn't seem to have any owner, but we've struck up a cautious friendship. For some reason, he looks for me every evening."

As if aware of being the center of conversation,

Beach appeared and strolled in their direction, stopping when he realized that Mason was not alone.

He sat slowly, watching Lianne with wary eyes. His gaze did not waver.

"Come, it's time for us to head back to the resort."

Mason placed his cane on the sand, using it to help rise to an erect position. She reached out to help him but immediately pulled back. She'd almost forgotten how proud men could be in situations like this.

With Beach a comfortable distance behind them, they headed back to the resort. Lianne wondered what had drawn the dog to the man, maybe because both of them were loners and survivors.

Lianne deliberately slowed the pace, faking tiredness, knowing that Mason would push himself, though he needed to moderate his regime.

"So have you been to any of the island's attractions since you arrived?" she asked.

"No, I've not been beyond the resort and this beach. I did plan to do a bit of it after I've settled and was a bit more mobile. I know the resort plans a trip or two every week."

"We went on a four-hour pleasure cruise on a schooner called the Jolly Roger. I haven't had so much fun in a long time. Each member of the crew was dressed like a pirate. They even made us walk the gangplank. I was so scared, but it was fun."

"I'd really like to visit some of the island, but I'd prefer to go on my own and not with the resort groups."

"Next week, we're going to Harrison's Cave, an underground cave that was rediscovered by two Barbadian in the late 1970s. But the cave is mentioned in history books dating as far back as the late 1700s. I can't wait to see it. I've been told that people say it should be one of the Seven Wonders of the World."

"You appear to have done your homework," he laughed.

"Not really. The resort provides all of the information and brochures needed. I hope you come with us. It'll be fun. I'm sure Mrs. Clarkson won't mind."

"I'll think about it and let you know, but it should be a lot of fun."

Lianne marveled at how he said this. *Doesn't appear that he had much fun in his life.*

They'd reached the perimeter of the resort and Beach stopped. Mason turned to the dog and spoke gently. "Later, my boy," he said, as if speaking to a close friend. "I'll see you in the morning. I'm sure we'll have some bacon and sausages for breakfast, so I'll bring something for you to eat."

Beach walked forward, licked Mason's hand and then turned and sprinted off, lost in the darkness.

"So you've made a friend on the island."

"Melissa, Mr. Buchanan's daughter, has been trying to befriend him, but no luck. For some reason, I'm the only one he trusts."

"At least he trusts someone."

"I'm thinking maybe he sees a bit of me in him. We're both lonely vagabonds."

"Yeah, both of you don't find it easy to trust."

"True. But since you seem to want to stay here and examine my psyche, I think it's time I go."

"I have to be going, too. I'm feeling a bit tired and recently Damien won't fall asleep unless I wish him good-night."

"You have a good night. I should probably go to the bar, drink a few beers and drown my sorrows, but since I don't drink I'll probably just have a cappuccino or latte. I've been told that the ones at the bar are great."

"They are. You have my word."

"Good, that's great." He paused. "Lianne, I wanted to say something before you go. Please accept my apologies for my abrupt exit the other night. I didn't mean to be rude."

"I understand. There's no need for an apology."

They'd reached the elevator and Mason pressed the button for her floor. When it arrived, he moved aside, allowing her to enter.

"Enjoy your night," he said and she watched as he disappeared even before the door of the lift closed.

* * *

The man placed the file on the desk and quickly scanned it. Agent Thomas and Smart were two of the agents assigned the case, he'd been informed, but the paper trail was petering out. There was something he needed to do, but the information he needed was hard to come by and time was moving fast.

He flicked another page and read as much as he could, but there was no information about Sheila Clarkson and her son's whereabouts. They'd somehow fallen off the face of the earth, but he had one more trick up his sleeve.

He could no longer think of the light. He'd embraced the darkness, realizing what had been missing from his life—this awesome sense of power and control.

He would stop at nothing to discover where Sheila and Damien Clarkson had been taken…. Even if it meant killing. That minor obstacle no longer bothered him.

His lack of success in finding the two runaways could mean the loss of his own family. The people who'd contacted him knew him well. His wife and children were the most important people in his life.

He'd kill to save them.

Chapter 6

Lianne prepared for dinner with the care of a woman knowing that she wanted to look good. She was looking forward to the night out. Yes, they'd be remaining on the property, but the restaurant on the beach would be without the screeching painful cry of the karaoke singers from several nights ago.

Slipping into one of the few semiformal dresses she'd brought with her, Lianne took a brief glimpse in the mirror. The dress was white and simply made. Body-hugging, it emphasized her slender but firm body. Lianne knew she looked good.

She added a pale red lipstick, a hint of green around

her eyes and she was ready. Pleased at her efforts, she reached for her bag and headed for the door.

When she arrived in the lobby, Sheila was waiting for her. She too looked beautiful. A pale green, the dress complimented her figure.

"Hi, let's us girls go enjoy a night out. I left the babysitter reading to Damien. He'll be soon fast asleep. The island air has that effect on him."

As they walked out the door and along the pathway that led to the restaurant, they were both oblivious of the picture they made and the numerous glances in their direction. Two stunning women, both tall, slender and beautiful. One, the soft shade of caramel; the other, the dark brown of the mahogany trees that grew in abundance on the island.

As they neared the restaurant, the steady beat of steel pans could be heard. When they reached the entrance, the hostess led them to a table close to where the music of the pounding surf in the distance could be heard. Leaving the menus, she retreated, promising to return as soon as they were ready.

"This is lovely," Sheila said. "I'm going to make sure that we return here someday. I wish Jason were here with us. It'd be perfect." Lianne heard the sadness in her voice. "But that's not what tonight is all about. We're here to enjoy ourselves. I can't help worrying about my husband, but I can't stay sulking in my room for the rest of the time here. I have to trust that Jason will be safe."

"He's safe. Our best men are protecting him. Nothing will happen to him. We're doing everything in our power to keep him alive."

"I know. Come, let's order. I'm going to have the Exotic Wild Rice and Honeyed Flying Fish Delight. My mouth is watering just thinking about eating it."

"Sounds great. I've been trying all of the local dishes. I'll have the same thing."

They waved to the hostess who immediately made her way toward them.

At the same time a very pregnant woman entered, scanned the restaurant and, without waiting for a hostess, headed to the empty table next to theirs. As she sat, she glanced at them, her smile warm and genuine.

A waitress immediately came to her table and said, "Good night, Mrs. Buchanan, welcome back home. Is Mr. Buchanan joining you?"

"No, he won't be. He did promise me dinner tonight, but there's a serious problem he has to deal with, so I'm all alone. I'll just have my favorite."

When the waitress left, the woman turned in their direction.

"I don't wish to be rude. But I really don't feel like eating on my own tonight. So how about I invite two of my guests to dinner and let us girls talk about clothes, or men."

At the shock on their faces, she burst into laughter. "I'm just kidding. I'm a happily married woman."

Lianne couldn't help but smile, and glanced in Sheila's direction, noticing immediately that the other woman was also smiling.

"Sure, we'd be glad for the company. How can we refuse a free meal with the owner's wife?"

"Oh, thank you. I couldn't bear the thought of eating alone. Thank you for having mercy on a lonely woman like me."

She stood gracefully and slipped into one of the empty chairs, a wide smile on her face.

"Sorry, let me introduce myself. As if you haven't already guessed. Alana Buchanan, the wife of the owner of this lovely resort and the mother of the little girl I'm sure you've seen running around the resort at a hundred miles per hour."

"I'm Sheila Blake and this is my son's nanny, Lianne."

Lianne breathed a sigh of relief. She'd remembered to use the assumed name.

"It's nice to meet both of you and thanks again for tolerating me for the evening."

"The pleasure is ours," Lianne said.

"So what are the two of you having for dinner? I noticed you've already made your choice. I'm

having the Exotic Wild Rice and Honeyed Flying
Fish Delight. That's the only thing my husband will
allow me to eat."

When both Lianne and Sheila burst out laughing,
she looked around, her eyes flickering around the
restaurant. Seeing nothing, she turned to them, an
eyebrow raised.

"Oh, dear, don't tell me I've said something silly."

"No, it's just that we ordered the same thing."

She laughed, a soft pleasant sound.

"So we'll have to go with that saying," she said.
"Great minds think alike."

Alana signaled to the hostess, who immediately
came and took her order. When that was done, she
turned to them.

"So how are you enjoying your stay on the
island?" she asked. "The Sunrise Resort is just over
a year old and we're already booked full for the
upcoming tourist season."

"I didn't realize that the resort was so new. You
have a great crowd already. I don't wish to be rude,
but don't I detect an American accent?"

"Yes, I'm from Reading, Pennsylvania. I came
to the island almost two years ago. Taurean and I
ended up staying in the same beach house because
of a mix-up. We fell in love and the rest is history.
We've been married just over a year. Let's see, it's
September. We've been married exactly seventeen

months and as you can see, I'm expecting our first child. Melissa's from my first husband."

Lianne heard the hint of sadness in her voice, but did not ask.

"The baby is due in a week or two. I was staying at a beach house we own for a few days. I had a painting I wanted to finish before the big event. Now, I can concentrate on having this baby."

"You must be looking forward to this baby."

"Oh, yes, we are. The baby's a blessing. I thank God daily for sending me Taurean," she said with the glow of a woman who was very much in love. "So, how are you enjoying the island? Beautiful, isn't it?"

"I've always loved Barbados. I was here a few years ago and once when I was in my teens, so it feels like coming home," Lianne replied.

"Me, either, and the beaches. I can't get enough of the sea," Sheila added. "My son, Damien, would live in the water all day now Lianne is teaching him how to swim. He was in the bathtub tonight practicing his strokes."

"He reminds me of Melissa when she first came to the island. She would stay on the beach, swim and collect shells all day if I allowed her to. Her best friends, Karen and Kerry, are no better. All three of them were born to be mermaids."

"Well, I could become a mermaid, too, if I lived on an island as beautiful as this one."

"It's an artist's paradise," Alana added. "All the paintings I've done in the past two years have been done here."

Sheila let out a scream. "You're *A. Buchanan!* Oh, my God. I remember hearing about you and going to your show when it debuted in New York. Your *Birth of a Hero* is totally awesome! No wonder you seemed familiar."

"Thank you. The island has been an inspiration."

"I don't know much about art, but you must let me see some of your work," Lianne said.

Alana was about to respond when the waitress arrived with their meals.

For a while there was no talking, only the gentle clang of knives against forks and the sighs and oohs and aahs of three women enjoying a great dinner. As they ate, each was in her own thoughts.

Lianne watched each woman as she ate, feeling a strange camaraderie with them. Working in a man's world didn't give her time to develop friendships with other sistahs, but she hoped it could be different now. At least, with Alana. There was something about the tiny pregnant woman that she found appealing. Sheila, she wasn't sure, since witness protection would be a must after the trial was over. Cordoni's influence was far reaching, even if he was in prison.

But, tonight was not a time to think of those

things. Lianne just intended to enjoy the night with her two new friends.

"So, who's in for some karaoke when we're finished eating? I feel like singing," Alana asked suddenly.

Yes, tonight, Lianne intended to have fun. What could be more fun than another night of off-key singers!

Saturday took longer to arrive than Carolyn anticipated. Filled with dread, she almost literally sat by the phone waiting for the call that seemed to take too long to come. But along with the dread was the anticipation at meeting the man who'd taken control of her every waking hour. She didn't like it one bit, losing control. There were still reservations about what she was about to do, despite her excitement at going on the date. For some reason she felt that she needed to put the two men from her past to rest. Until she did this, she could not move forward. For some reason, she'd somehow linked them to her happiness.

On Friday afternoon while she sat reading her favorite author's latest release, she had almost given up hope that he'd call.

And then the call came, his voice over the line as arresting as in person.

"Carolyn is that you? This is Garth Wade."

"Hi, how're you doing? I really didn't expect you to call—" Okay, I'm lying she thought "—but I'm glad to hear from you."

"Oh, so you didn't expect me to call." He laughed as if he knew she were lying, but Carolyn remained silent.

"So why didn't you expect me to call? Oh, I won't ask you to respond. I do, however, have bad news for you. The dean of my faculty was scheduled to attend a seminar for the next four days in Florida, but he has taken ill and I have to attend in his place. I won't be back until Tuesday."

Carolyn tried to hide her disappointment. "I understand. I'm glad you called to let me know."

"I just wanted to let you know before I leave for the airport. I leave in a few minutes. I know you didn't give me your number but I checked the directory and it was there."

She placed his mind at rest and reassured him that dinner could wait until he returned.

With that he said goodbye and was gone.

For the rest of the day, Carolyn sat and sulked, unable to deal with her disappointment.

I'm just a drama queen. I really need to pull myself out of this.

The seed of an idea formed in her mind and before she knew it she was dialing American Airlines to ask for the schedule to Chicago. She would go and see

Joshua's grave and spend a few days in the city. She'd wondered what had happened to Joshua all those years ago and was sure she'd be able to find out some information about him and his family.

She wondered if he'd ever completed college as he'd wanted. When he disappeared, she knew her parents had intervened. Not because his family didn't have money, but because her mother had dreamed of Carolyn marrying a white man. When Joshua had threatened her years of careful planning, his family's wealth and reputation did not matter. Her mother had been thrilled that John had been willing to marry her, despite the pregnancy.

All Carolyn knew was that Joshua had returned home. He had not fought for her. Marrying John Sinclair had provided a choice she could not refuse, so she'd married him.

The day after Garth had called, she boarded the American Airlines flight, arriving in Chicago several hours later and checked into the Westin Chicago River North Hotel.

Early the next morning as Carolyn sat on the balcony of her hotel room, she wondered if she was doing the right thing. The need to visit Joshua's grave had been overwhelming and she knew that she needed to put him to rest if she wanted to go on with her life.

Ironically, Joshua's passing had finally forced her to jump off the never-ending ride of her current existence. Shame washed over her as she thought of the meaningless liaisons that had become so much a part of her life.

Now, her life was filled with possibilities. Garth was nothing like the men she'd sought out. She'd avoided the intellectual type, who reminded her of her late husband. And definitely, none that looked like Joshua.

Instead, she preferred the safety of empty-headed young men whose main purpose for living was to look pretty, enhance their already muscular physiques and prey on rich lonely women.

Like her.

And she'd been a willing participant in their false promises of love and happily-ever-after. Returning to the U.S. was the most sensible thing she'd done since leaving for Europe four years ago.

Later that day, when the sun's rays gently touched the few trees in the cemetery she stood before Joshua's plot. The area around had already been landscaped, giving the appearance of having been there for years. The finality shocked her. What unrealistic hope she'd had that he'd not passed away became the image of him locked in the box.

As she sat and stared at it, she remembered the time, the relationship and her broken dreams.

Her liaison with Joshua had continued for several months. She remembered clearly the night they'd made love for the first time. It had been fast and intense and she'd felt that she could never have enough of the man who'd caused her to sin, but they were young and the lust of the flesh was more than they could handle. Two or more times a day they'd made love to each other, both bothered by the guilt of sex outside of marriage. Despite constant prayer, they could not keep their hands off each other.

But all that stopped three months later when Carolyn realized that her unsettled stomach was a result of her pregnancy.

Somehow her mother had realized and, before Carolyn could tell Joshua the good news, he'd disappeared. A few weeks later, she'd been shipped off to an aunt living in the South. Mason Joshua Sinclair had been born four months later, the spitting image of his father.

John had come along and she'd quickly married and settled into a life of marital contentment.

Now, as she stood before the gravestone of the man she'd loved more than life itself, her years of anger faded. He'd been a young man then and she'd been just as young and faced with parents and a situation she could not handle. Her mother, always a formidable opponent, would have made minced meat out of the youthful Joshua. On reflection, Carolyn knew she had no choice but to forgive the sins of others. She, for one, had not been spotless.

Life was so strange with its constant changes.

At this age, when she should be comfortable and contented with her life, a man ten years younger had upset her comfortable existence.

Carolyn was torn about what to do.

She looked at Joshua's gravestone and for a moment she saw him, the tall handsome young man who'd taught her the joy and excitement of loving. She lowered herself, kneeling before him.

For a moment she was sixteen again—a young, vulnerable girl with stars in her eyes and exciting plans for the future. In one night, however, that had changed. The magical quality of the fairy-tale romance had disappeared with the stirring of the new life inside her.

As Carolyn knelt, the tears began to flow, and she cried for young love and dreams.

She told Joshua about his son and how much his son looked like him. She told him about John and the happy life she'd had for a while, and she told him about Garth and the fear and apprehension she felt at falling in love again. Carolyn knew she was falling.

When she left the cemetery, she felt better, as if a weight had been lifted off her shoulders.

Now all she had to do was enjoy the ride with Garth Wade.

Lianne closed the door behind her and headed down the stairs to the lobby. Sheila and Damien were in their room, and Brent, Smart and Monroe, in position in the room just next door, would make sure nothing went wrong. Already the necessary surveillance equipment linking the rooms had been installed.

Lianne was glad, since it gave her a chance to take a break from the stress of taking care of Sheila and Damien. It was only when she left them for an hour or so that she realized the stress of being constantly in their presence. Away from them, her body noticeably relaxed, the tension released with the disappearance of a constant headache that did not want to go away.

When she reached the lobby, she turned left, exiting the building from a door that led to the side of the hotel away from the beach.

Someone had told her that beyond the resort lay a tiny woodland area in which remnants of the island's natural foliage and wildlife could still be seen. She wondered where Mason was. She'd have loved him to join her on the journey. Somehow she had an idea that he'd enjoy seeing some of the island's naturalness.

As she moved away from the resort, the terrain lost its orderliness and the slightly untamed look of the woodland area replaced it. When she reached the edge of the woodland area, she hesitated but remembered that management had said it was safe to enter since most of the wildlife was harmless.

Lianne entered, unaware of the man who walked slowly behind her.

Mason watched as Lianne moved quickly across the gardens of the resort. She seemed to be heading in the direction of a wooded area just beyond the tennis courts. Ironically, he'd planned to explore the area, since mention had been made of a clearing somewhere inside the area where a small spring made its way down to the sea.

He increased his speed as much as was possible, but slowed when he realized it would be too much strain on his leg to try to reach her. He'd meet her eventually if she followed the path and arrows directing the way.

As he walked, he whistled the now familiar song of one of the island's most popular calypsos. The sun was hot, not a burning heat, but one that allowed him to be easily cooled by the ocean breeze wafting off the waves he could hear in the distance.

Following the path Lianne had taken, he went farther and farther into the woods, occasionally passing an individual or group returning from their own tour of the area.

He cleared a thick canopy of leaves above and stepped into what must have been one of the most beautiful spots on the island.

Before him, water sparkled and glistened under the rays of the sun as the stream made its way along the rocky bed toward the sea.

He glanced around, his gaze landing on Lianne where she sat overlooking a waterfall that cascaded into a tiny pool below where happy brown ducks dived in and out of the water.

He heard the tinkle of her laughter, an animated sound that came from deep within her and echoed in the silence of the clearing.

A rustling of leaves forced him to look up as two monkeys swung by, leaping from tree to tree, ignoring the humans below.

He could not help but laugh. At the sound, Lianne turned in his direction, a startled look on her face. When she recognized him, a wide smile touched her lips. She had a way of making him feel special, wanted.

Mason tried to calm himself, but the need to be with her was overwhelming. No, he couldn't wait to be with her.

When he reached her, he was at a loss for words, feeling as if he were sixteen and on his first date.

"If I knew you were planning to come here, I would have come along with you. This place is too beautiful not to share. I was thinking that just before you appeared."

"Ironically, I was heading here when I saw you just ahead of me. Of course, with my reduced speed I couldn't catch up and I didn't want to shout. I suspected you'd be here. Everyone has been talking about this secluded spot."

"I'm not sure if we can call it secluded with so many of the guests coming here during the day. It must be lovely at night."

"Is that an invitation to come here one night with you? I could come with you if you're scared of the dark and things that go bump in the night. I'm not sure if I'd want to come here at night by myself," Mason cautioned.

"I'm sure you have nothing to be worried about. The hotel's brochure says that there are lights on until ten o'clock each night."

"Oh, maybe we could come for a picnic?"

"If you wish. Once you're preparing the food and it's just you and I."

"I was thinking about bringing Sheila and Damien along," she teased. "As chaperones, so you don't get naughty."

"Oh, I have no problem with that. I have no intentions of being naughty. I've always been a good boy."

"That's good to know."

Mason realized that somehow their simple flirtation had become a deep awareness of each other and the mutual attraction had slowly become a consuming desire for each other.

"For some strange reason, I'm not sure I don't want to be a bad boy right now. I've always wondered why women find bad boys so fascinating."

"This may be a good time to find out." Lianne's heart quickened as his face moved closer. She closed her eyes, already feeling his lips on hers. When their mouths did touch, it was all and more than she'd expected. A flash of lightning surged through her body and she almost pulled away with its intensity.

The kiss was no gentle caress of her lips as she'd anticipated but a cry of desperation and a powerful need to be a part of each other. It did not bring images of roses, but an image of their bodies entwined and her legs wrapped around him.

When she felt his withdrawal, her eyes opened.

"Seems like we have observers."

She glanced in the direction of his gaze and laughed when she saw a pair of rabbits staring at them.

"I'm sure they're just jealous and about to do the same thing."

"I think it's time we go. It's soon time for dinner, and I don't want to be late. The crowd can get long at the buffet table if you're not there on time. Want to join me for dinner?"

"I'd love to."

Lianne rose and held her hand out to help Mason up. He accepted her assistance. She tried not to look surprised.

"I may be proud, even a bit macho at times, but I'm definitely not crazy. I know my current limitations. Why exacerbate it by struggling to get up?"

Lianne smiled. Mason never ceased to amaze her. Despite his handicap, he exuded confidence and strength, making his need to carry a cane more of an extension of who he was instead of a limitation.

They walked in silence, each enjoying the stillness of the surroundings.

It was only when they reached the entrance of the resort that they realized they were holding hands.

An hour later, Mason stared at the image in the mirror and was pleased by what he saw. The pair of loose white slacks he wore did nothing to hide the firm muscles of his legs. The close-fitting Dolce & Gabbona shirt too did little to hide the hint of a firm six-pack that he worked out in the gym to maintain. Now, he tried to confine his exercise to his walking and the countless sit-ups he still did routinely each morning.

Slipping on a tan pair of loafers, he left the room and headed downstairs to the indoor restaurant that beckoned each night with its spicy aroma. He'd preferred to eat in his room or in the less formal restaurant on the beach, but he wanted tonight to be different, so he'd called Lianne and asked her to dress up.

And dress up she did!

When he exited the elevator, his eyes immediately found hers. As usual, the smile on her face gave rise to his now customary warring feelings.

He didn't know much about what women wore, but the white dress she had on hugged her body in all of the right places.

"Sorry, it took me so long," he said when he reached her. "I received a call just as I was about to go in the bath. My late partner's wife and kids. I had to talk to the girls. They miss their dad."

Lianne stared at him. Mason Sinclair was really a special man and didn't even realize it.

"Come, let's go before the restaurant fills up."

She complied when he took her hand, enjoying the warmth of his touch.

When they reached the entrance of the restaurant, the hostess took them immediately to a table by a window overlooking the grounds of the resort. In the distance, the breaking waves of the sea could be seen.

Taking a look at the menus, their order of dinner was quickly given to the hostess and for a while they sat watching as the moon peeped from beyond the horizon. A flock of birds, seeming late for their bedtime, flew swiftly by, disappearing into the branches of the mahogany trees that could be seen all over the resort.

"I've traveled to many places, but it's only in Barbados that I really feel at home. I love the island. If there was anywhere else I would live, Barbados would get my vote," Lianne said.

"I know the feeling. I've never been here before, but I'm amazed at its beauty. I plan to go on a few of the tours before I leave."

"You must. There are several places that are worth seeing. Harrison's Cave, the museum, Welchman Hall Gully."

"You've been to the island before?"

Before the question came, Lianne had realized her mistake. "When I was in my teens, my parents used to bring us to Barbados every summer. So when Mrs. Clarkson was looking for somewhere to bring Damien, I suggested here."

Before he could respond, the waiter came with their meal and conversation stopped until they were served.

"One thing I must say is that the food here is wonderful. The chef is a wonder."

"I totally agree. Each of the restaurants have their own distinct style and taste, but this is excellent. I've eaten at restaurants all over the world, but this is by far one of my favorites."

While they ate, between savoring the delicious local flying fish, their conversation ranged from movies to sports, music and art. In the background, the soothing sound of the steel pan helped to create the perfect mood for lovers.

When the meal was over, feeling pleasantly content, Mason asked if she'd like to go for a stroll in the resort's gardens.

Lianne agreed, knowing that there was a sense of promise, of anticipation, of excitement.

Mason reached for her hand again as they strolled through the dimly lit garden. He stopped in the shade of a dense mahogany tree and pulled her into his arms. She moved willingly to comply.

There was no need for conversation. They both knew why they were here. The kiss earlier had held promise and they both wanted to explore that hint of excitement, the possibilities of passion and fulfillment.

When their lips touched this time, it was the same, but different.

Now, there was a sense of familiarity, but this did not lessen the effect of the heat surging through Mason's body. Her lips tasted like the warm honey he loved to put on his pancakes. When Lianne groaned, he lost control, his erection straining against her womanhood.

The kiss deepened and he knew he could never get enough of her. Already he knew it was more than just a physical need. The unexpected stirring of something deeper scared him, but he couldn't help himself. There was something about Lianne Thomas that made him think of forever.

He became aware of her hands around him, gripping his behind and pulling him closer to her. He could feel every curve of her body and the firm pebbles of her nipples against his chest. He gently pushed her away, turning her around and resting her back against the trunk of the tree. Their eyes locked and he smiled.

"I've never met a woman I wanted so much. I need to touch you, taste you."

She didn't respond, but closed her eyes. He quickly lowered the straps of her dress, exposing her firm breasts. He lowered his head, taking the left one in his mouth and feeling the telltale jerk of response. Lianne groaned, a groan that only served to make him even hornier.

Satisfied that the first breast had been taken care

of, he moved to the next one, teasing it between his teeth.

Lianne raised his head, pulling him to her, and he kissed her again.

This time, the kiss cried of desperation and unfulfilled love.

"Damn, I could kiss you all night. And you know I want to make love to you, but I'm not ready yet, and I know you aren't. I want to do this right. Let's get to know each other. We'll both know when it's right. If it ever is? Let's go sit on the bench over there. Talk. I want to hear some more about your travels."

Lianne did not respond. She only followed him. Inside, warring emotions and the intensity of their actions had taken its toll, creating an ache inside that threatened to drive her crazy.

But yes, she'd sit and talk. Being around Mason Sinclair was more than a pleasure.

What scared Lianne most what that she knew she was falling in love.

Hopelessly and dangerously in love.

Carolyn turned the key in the lock and stepped into her apartment where she now lived. Tossing her handbag on the closest chair, she walked immediately to her answering machine, pressed the flashing messages button and listened to the few that had been left. One from the hospital where she volunteered and another from her lawyer. As she checked the final call, her heart beat in anticipation.

Garth's deep baritone filled the room with its intensity. "Carolyn, I just wanted to let you know how sorry I am that I can't be there. I was looking forward to our day together. I'm on my way to a workshop I have to attend. I'll try to reach you later tonight or tomorrow."

It was only when she felt the rush of air that she realized she'd been holding her breath. What was happening to her? Her heart was fluttering like a trapped butterfly and she knew that she was also weakening. Garth Wade was slowly working himself under her skin and she didn't like it one bit.

What she needed to do was take a bath to clear her head!

She headed straight for the bathroom and slipped out of the outfit she wore. Before she stepped into the tub, she glanced at herself in the mirror.

What she saw did not totally displease her, but she wondered how a man ten years her junior would react.

Though she exercised regularly, time had touched her, gently, but had touched her. Her waist had lost its neatness and her breasts were not as firm as they had been. She tentatively touched one breast, imagining Garth's lips on her.

Immediately, she pulled herself from her erotic

musing, knowing that she'd only frustrate herself in the meantime. She knew that eventually they would make love, but this incessant obsession with him could prove to be her downfall.

And Carolyn Sinclair never lost control.

She moved away from the mirror quickly, stepped into the shower, and forced herself to think of anything but the man who now haunted her dreams.

Chapter 7

Mason could not believe that the day had passed so quickly. He looked forward to the evening, since he knew he would see Lianne again. He'd enjoyed his time with her yesterday—their time in the woods and the kisses.

Definitely, the kisses.

He looked out the window, noticing his niece waving at Bertha Gooding as she drove away in a red Suzuki Vitara. Melissa watched until the car disappeared around the corner before she headed in the direction of the beach.

He felt the urge to go chat with his niece. Maybe

she'd give him some insight into what kind of person his brother was.

He quickly put his shoes on, left his room and headed for the beach. He'd planned to go in the water today since the occasional swim would help to strengthen his legs.

Minutes later when he approached Melissa where she was frantically digging, she looked up and on seeing him squealed in excitement.

"Mr. Sinclair, how are you? I've been wondering if you're still at the resort. I only came back home this morning. My best friends, Karen and Kerry, returned from Trinidad and I went to spend the weekend with them. Their mother just left. They're coming to spend the weekend with me and I'm so excited. I can't wait. We're going to make some jewelry."

"Seems to me that one day you're going to open your own business."

"Oh, well, I'm really not sure what I want to be. Once I wanted to be a dancer and then I wanted to be an athlete and just last week I wanted to be a model. Tyra Banks is just fab-u-lous, isn't she?"

Mason laughed. "So am I to assume that in the next few days you're going to want to be something else?"

"Oh, I'm sure I'll want to be. Right now, I'm very in-de-ci-sive. Did I use that word correctly? I only learned it yesterday when I was reading. Mommy says that reading helps to build your vocabulary, so I try to learn as many new words as possible."

Again, Mason laughed. His niece was such a delightful child and smart, too.

"What kind of work, do you do?" she asked when she stopped giggling. "I hope I'm not being rude."

"No, you're not. The only way you can learn things and understand is by asking questions."

"You sound just like my dad, but he also says, 'Melissa, you never ask questions that are too personal,' in his try-to-sound-serious voice."

"He's right, but that's an easy question to answer and I don't think you're being personal. Before my accident, I was an FBI agent."

"An agent? Does that mean you were some kind of cop?"

"Yeah, in a way. I was a special type of cop. I go after really, really bad people in the U.S."

She was silent for a moment as if thinking about what to say.

"Is that how you hurt your leg?"

"Yes, I did. I was trying to save my partner, but he died. He was the best agent I know."

"I'm sorry. My real daddy died, too, but Taurean adopted me and now I'm a Buchanan. I love my

new daddy and my uncle Patrick and auntie Paula.
She's Patrick's wife. She's so much fun. And I like
my uncle Daniel, too. He always looks serious and
doesn't like to have fun. But he's still really nice.
His wife just had a baby son. I saw a picture of the
baby and he's really, really tiny." Her voice went to
a whisper. "And he's not too cute."

"My, you have a large family."

"Do you have brothers and sister, too?" she asked.

He wasn't sure how to answer but decided not
to lie. He wouldn't say too much.

"Yes, I have brothers but my dad died just like
yours."

"I'm sorry to hear that. Do you miss your dad?"

"Yes, he was my best friend."

"I don't miss my other dad, but my new dad,
Taurean, is my best friend, too. Karen and Kerry are
my best friends that are girls. I can be your friend,
too. You look sad sometimes."

Mason was unsure of how to respond to Melissa's
intuition. She seemed mature beyond her years.

Before he could reply, he heard a voice shouting
for Melissa.

His brother.

"Melissa, I'm leaving shortly to collect Karen and
Kerry. Remember, they are staying the night. And
your mom is having a guest for dinner. You need to
clean up your room a bit and get in the shower."

When Melissa ran off with a "Goodbye, Mr. Sinclair!" her father, his brother, turned to him. Mason saw the flash of wariness in Taurean's eyes.

"I'm sorry I kept her back," Mason explained. "She asked me to help her find shells." Again, he saw the slight mistrust.

"You have no need to worry," he added. "She's safe with me."

The two men looked at each other, assessing what each other's face revealed.

"I usually don't allow Melissa to associate too often with the guests. You must be careful these days."

Again, Mason felt the surge of anger, but he understood his brother's reasoning.

"I understand, Mr. Buchanan. I'll make sure I keep a comfortable distance in the future. I did not realize I was causing her to disobey your rules. For that I am truly sorry. It was not my intention to cause any trouble."

His brother continued to look at him.

"No harm done. I'll be going." He moved to walk away and then stopped, turning slowly to face Mason.

"Come to my house tonight for dinner. My wife has invited a friend over. So have mercy on me, come over, let's drink a few beers and if you play pool, I have a table in the basement."

"I play pool," Mason responded. His immediate response surprised him, since his brother's initial reaction left a bitter taste, but this was an opportunity he could not refuse. "Yes, I'll come."

"Good, I should be apologizing, too. I don't usually jump to conclusions, but I love my daughter and I'll do anything to protect her. Our home is the gray house just beyond the lawn tennis courts. I'll look for you around seven."

"Thank you again. I'll be there."

Mason watched as his brother walked briskly away. Long strides that hinted at the power of the man.

Taurean didn't look as Mason had expected him to. His brother was big and well-built, but carried himself with a grace and agility that surprised and seemed at odds with his size.

Taurean's dark complexion reminded him of the mahogany trees that dotted the grounds of the resort. Mason could see that he and his brother took after their father. Though his skin was a few tones lighter, a dark caramel, their eyes had been painted with the same unusual brandy shade that his mother had always claimed came from his father's side of the family.

Now, with those eyes, he watched his brother enter the simple but elegant two-story house surrounded by swaying palm trees.

Seven o'clock. Tonight promised to be an intriguing one. He couldn't wait.

* * *

The phone roused Carolyn from the sleep that had taken her into the world of the erotic. For the past few nights she'd been visited by the man himself, the youthful professor, always tempting her with his wonderful lovemaking, until she woke up in the middle of the night, aching for his hands on her.

Who on earth could be calling her so early in the morning? Most of her friends knew that she didn't like to get up early.

She lifted the receiver reluctantly.

"Carolyn, I hope I didn't wake you from sleeping." She could hear the hint of laughter in his voice. Of course, he knew she'd be awake, but she loved his brash boldness.

"So how's my favorite girl?"

She laughed. "*Girl,* I've stopped being a girl so many years ago. But if by chance you mean me, I'm doing quite fine."

"That's good to know. I'm calling to invite you out tonight to dinner. I'd like you to come with me."

Carolyn hesitated.

"I'd love to," slipped from her.

"Good, I have a little surprise in store."

"Oh," she replied. She was curious. She wondered about the surprise.

"What time do you want me to be ready?"

"Six o'clock. I'll pick you up. You just need to let me know where you live."

She rattled off directions to her home.

"Oh, you're quite close to me. I just live about two miles to the south."

"So we're almost neighbors."

"Seems that we are. Well, that settles it. I'll see you this evening, honey. I have to go. I have an early call."

Carolyn loved the sound of her name on Garth's lips, but the word *honey* sent shivers down her spine with its hint of intimacy and warmth.

"I'll be ready," she said.

"I can't wait to see you. Enjoy the rest of your day," he said and she heard the click of the phone.

Immediately, she moved into action. First the hairdresser and then a new dress. Although he'd not said, she assumed the dinner would be formal. And she really didn't want to wear anything she had in her current wardrobe.

Picking up the phone, she quickly called her hairstylist.

Several hours later, her hair glowing under the neon lights, she sashayed into her favorite boutique on Main Street. One of the sales assistants immediately came to take care of her. In Georgio's store, customers didn't shop, they were pampered and allowed to take away one of his creations…for a price.

"Mrs. Sinclair, it's great to see you. We haven't seen you for a while."

"Hi, Angie. I've been in Europe. I'm sure you can help me. I need the perfect dress for tonight. I have a formal dinner to go to and I want to be the belle of the ball."

"You're in luck. We've only just placed several new dresses on the racks today. There's a perfectly delightful green dress that has your name written on it."

As Carolyn looked at herself in the mirror several minutes later, she realized that the dress was indeed perfect. It hugged her like a second skin, making her look years younger.

"I'll take it," she told Angie.

"Good, it's perfect on you. Go to the lounge and have a cup of coffee or tea. I'll have it ready in a minute."

"Thank you, Angie. You've saved my life."

"Well, you know we're always here to please."

Carolyn moved into the tiny lounge that had been set up for customers. She lifted one of the croissants and poured a glass of the ice-cold lemonade for which Georgio's was also known.

Driving home a few minutes later, her thoughts turned to the man who was constantly on her mind. She hoped the dress would create the reaction she anticipated it would. Garth Wade was in for a night he wouldn't forget.

Was she falling in love? No, she couldn't allow that to happen. She knew the pain of losing someone you loved, and for the past few years her dalliances had been enough.

But Garth had her thinking of things she'd dared not wish for or want.

What was happening to her? It was not that she missed the touch of a man. She had lovers.

But she wanted more. She missed the easy companionship with John. The knowledge that someone was there to share your problems and your life. Someone to wake up next to in the morning.

When she'd finished eating, she took her time dressing, wanting to make sure she looked her best.

For an hour she lay in the bathtub making sure. She felt invigorated when she slipped out of the water.

Later, when she walked downstairs and stood waiting by the window, she knew she looked good.

Mason walked slowly over to his brother's home, the light of the house beckoning him. *Apprehension* was the word he'd use to describe how he was feeling at the moment. He knew that after tonight he would have to make a decision that could affect not only his life but the lives of his brothers and his mother.

Already the sun had set and, perched between

the clouds, a slice of moon peeked out, its weak beam providing very little light.

Though apprehensive, Mason looked forward to the visit to his brother's house. He knew his brother had done some checking. He'd received a call from one of his former agents informing him that a Taurean Buchanan had called about him. At first Mason had been angry, but on reflection he'd realized that his brother had only been protecting his daughter, something Mason knew he would do if placed in the same situation.

He reached the house and heard laughter coming from inside. He pressed the door bell and the thunder of footsteps echoed inside.

Melissa.

The door flew open and there she stood with two girls. The twins. He wondered how anyone could tell them apart.

"Mr. Sinclair, Mommy said to come right in. Oh, forgive me. These are my two best friends—Karen and Kerry."

The two girls giggled, a twinkle of four very bright eyes staring at him. He could tell that they were a handful.

And then his brother appeared, an apron around his waist. Taurean wore it with an air of confidence.

"Come in, Mason. I've been assigned the cook for the night so you can join me in the kitchen. The girls will entertain themselves. Alana and her friend are in the sitting room."

Mason followed his brother down the corridor and into the kitchen. The room was warm and stark-white, making it seem larger that it actually was.

"We usually eat in here, but since we have guests, we're going to use the dining room. The door opens onto a balcony with a perfect view of the ocean."

Suddenly, Mason didn't know what to say. He'd planned this evening for hours in his mind. He would be the cool, level-headed individual over-flowing with confidence. Already, he'd failed.

His brother broke the silence.

"If you can make a salad, the ingredients are on the counter over there."

"I'm quite handy in the kitchen. I have one of those mothers who believes that a man should be able to take care of himself in case he doesn't get married. I think she was trying to tell me in a smart way that it was time to move out," Mason responded.

His brother laughed, a deep husky sound that was pleasant to the ear. "You have a mother just like mine, though she believes that a man needs to be able to cook in order to attract a woman."

"Seems like it worked on Alana. You have a beautiful wife and daughter."

"I know. I've only been married for just over

one year. Alana was married before. Melissa is my stepdaughter, but I love her as if she were my own."

"I can see she's a handful, but smart for her age."

"Yes, she's totally different from the Melissa I met when I first came to the island. Both of them are different. I can only thank God that He brought them into my life."

There was a noise behind them and they turned together.

Alana stood there, a strange look in her eyes. Mason held her gaze for the briefest of moments. Somehow she suspected something. A look of mistrust entered her eyes, but her mouth curled in a smile.

She walked over to them, outstretching her hand just as she reached him.

"Hi, I'm Alana. So you're the man who has captured my daughter's heart. She's always talking about Mason. She just told me you've arrived. She and the twins are entertaining a friend of mine while I check on my husband's progress. Not that I need to. He's one of the better chefs I know. And I can see he's trying to make one out of you, too." She turned to Taurean. "How could you invite Mason over and then put him to prepare his own dinner?" she asked.

"Mason is more than a guest. He's Melissa's friend."

"Of course, I know he's more than a guest." There was a hint of teasing in her voice.

"Well, we must talk sometime, but I need to get back to my friend. Can't have the girls exhausting her before she has eaten."

"Yes, give me ten minutes. With Mason's help I'll be done in a flash."

Alana turned and walked away, but not before Mason saw the glint of awareness in her eyes.

Lianne watched as Alana entered the room. She could not help but admire how the woman carried herself. She'd never agreed with the claim that women looked more beautiful when they were pregnant, but there was something about Alana that sparkled, as if she were born to be a mother. Lianne watched how Alana handled Melissa and her two friends and wondered if she could ever be like that. She was sure she didn't have a maternal bone in her body.

"Dinner will soon be ready. You're in for an experience. Taurean is an excellent cook. Much better than I am," Alana said.

"A handsome husband and a cook. You're one lucky woman. I hope I'm that lucky if I get married," Lianne replied.

"If? You're not sure if you want to get married?"

"To be honest, I haven't thought about marriage

much. With my job and all the traveling, forming a relationship just isn't easy."

"But I'm sure you've met someone special in all the time you've traveled."

Mason came to mind. *Yes, she definitely met someone special.*

"Is that smile an indication that you've met someone here? I wonder who he is." The smirk on her face told Lianne that Alana must have seen them together.

"Okay, Alana, I'm sure you have an idea, but to be on the safe side, why don't you tell me about your art? I didn't even know you were famous."

"Famous! I'm far from being famous."

"If the paintings hanging in the resort and the few I see here are an indication of your talent, I'm definitely impressed."

"Most of the paintings in the resort are mine, but the ones you see here are done by Rommel Year-wood. He's quite young, but definitely talented. How'd you like to see my studio later? I don't show many people my work in progress but I'll make an exception."

"You don't have to do that," Lianne said.

"Oh, think nothing of it. I'd like you to see what I'm working on. And of course, I'll show you some of Melissa's work. She's extremely talented. Much more than I was at her age."

"How old is Melissa? Ten, eleven?" Lianne asked.

"She turned ten a few months ago."

"She seems older, mature for her age."

"Melissa has had to grow up a lot in the last few years." Alana hesitated as if unsure of what to say. "I only met Taurean two years ago when I came to the island. I'd just been granted a divorce from my husband, but he was still harassing me. My best friend, Paula, is married to Taurean's brother and she let me use the beach house. I got fake passports and came to the island."

"I'm so sorry. That couldn't have been easy."

"No, it wasn't. Blake, my ex-husband, eventually found us here and tried to kill me, but Taurean saved us. In a struggle with Taureen, Blake fell off a cliff, and plunged to his death. I'd fallen for Taureen even before then. It took me a while before I could trust anyone. Taurean may be large and muscular, but he's one of the most sensitive persons I know."

"He is large isn't he? Strangely enough, he looks a bit like Mason, except that Mason is not as large. More lithe."

"I know what you mean. I've noticed it, too. They could easily pass for brothers."

"Yes, it's not totally in the look, but the way they move almost noiselessly, and the way they both look at you in this deep intense way."

"If Taurean's father had not been a priest, I'd wonder if he cheated."

Before Lianne could respond, Taurean entered the room, and the shadow of a man behind him morphed into Mason Sinclair.

Seeing them standing next to each other was the most amazing and eerie thing.

"We were just talking about how alike the two of you look, almost as if you could be brothers," Alana said, her gaze moving from her husband to Mason and then back.

Taurean laughed. "Come off it. We look nothing like each other. I'm massive in comparison to Mason."

But Taurean turned toward Mason, his eyes searching, still not registering the similarities.

"Oh, well, maybe we do look a bit alike, but right now, I'm so hungry I could eat all that food I've prepared on my own. I'm sure that everyone is hungry, too. So you ladies just go onto the balcony, Taurean and I will get everything. The girls are already eating in the kitchen."

Mason waited with Taurean until the ladies were seated and returned to the kitchen for the salad and soup they had prepared.

When they returned to the balcony, Lianne and Alana were already seated, their faces animated with laughter. The table had already been set and the other dishes had been placed on warmers to maintain their heat.

He'd been surprised to see Lianne here tonight. When he'd heard about Alana's friend, Lianne had been the last person on his mind. He hadn't even realized she and Alana had met.

Tonight, Lianne wore a simple black dress—if it could be called *simple*—that hugged her every curve, emphasizing her slender but well-toned physique.

When he lowered himself into the chair Taurean indicated, next to where Lianne sat, his leg brushed hers and the resulting flash of heat startled him. His body tensed, noticing the sudden heave of her breasts. The air crackled with tension and he saw the awareness in her eyes and knew he would lose this battle.

Counting to ten, he tried to regain his composure, glad when Taurean suggested giving thanks for the meal.

During the meal, however, Mason found himself glancing in her direction whenever he felt no one was looking. Somehow being with Alana had transformed Lianne into a more feminine version of the woman he saw every day. She laughed and giggled, her face animated with joy.

During dinner, he also found himself glancing at his brother and noticing particular mannerisms that were so familiar.

An hour later, he sat with Taurean alone on the balcony. Alana, with Lianne, had cleared the table, while he and Taurean had taken care of the kitchen. On their return to the balcony, Alana had announced that they, the ladies, were off to her studio, and that they, the men, were free to spend the rest of the night doing whatever they wanted.

They sat in silence, both immersed in their own thoughts, when Taurean finally spoke. "So you're not married?"

"No. Almost did years ago, but it didn't work out. I'm not sure I'm cut out for marriage."

"Never thought I would either since not many women want to marry an ex-con."

"You're an ex-con?"

"Yes, seven years. My brother was dying and I removed the life support. I spent seven years in prison. Came to Barbados about two years ago to adapt to the outside world again and fell in love with Alana. We married and decided to settle here."

"Man, you've had a hard life, but at least now you have a lovely family, a great home and run your own business. Not many men are that lucky to find happiness."

"I count my blessings every day. I have a wonderful wife, and daughter I love like she's my own, and a baby on the way. Yes, I'm happy."

"I can see that Melissa's special. She did tell me you're her stepdad."

"Yes, she's the joy of my life. I don't think I could live without either one of them."

Tauren paused for a moment before he asked the question Mason knew was coming.

"So what brings you to the island?" The question was simple, but Mason knew it went deeper.

"I'm...was an FBI agent, but I was injured in an accident about a few months ago, and spent some time recuperating. The island seemed the prefect place to relax and think about my future. I'm not even sure I want to be an agent anymore."

"Maybe it's time you settle down and get married."

"Me? Get married?" Mason said this with a touch of sarcasm, but Lianne's face flashed in front him.

"Lianne is a beautiful woman," Taurean said. "I noticed you can't keep your eyes off her."

"Yes, she is beautiful. Too beautiful for a nanny."

"If I weren't married, she could be my nanny any day, but I've found my soul mate."

For a moment they were silent.

"Taurean, there's something I need to show you. I didn't plan to but maybe telling you now is the right thing to do. I don't want to continue hiding this from you."

Mason stood, retrieving the document from his pocket. He handed it to his brother.

Taurean took the paper, unfolded it and read the report.

For a while, he was silent.

"How?" His brother finally spoke.

"My mother told me a few weeks ago. She saw his obituary in the newspaper and told me the truth. But she thought that just knowing would be enough for me. I just wanted to see who my brothers were. When the investigator told me that you lived here, I decided to come."

Taurean didn't respond. Mason could see the emotion on his face.

"I'm sorry I had to tell you like this. I don't want to cause any trouble. I'm not after anything. I just want to find out about my family, my brothers."

"I understand. I would have done the same thing." Taurean paused as if unsure of what he wanted to ask. "I just need to ask one question. How old are you?"

"Forty-two."

"Three years older than I am. I was born just ten months after my parents married. How could my father keep this secret all these years?"

"He didn't know about me. He left New York before my mother could tell him she was pregnant. My grandmother made sure that my mother couldn't have contact."

"Damn, this is so crazy. It's the biggest of ironies. And we were talking so much about how much we look alike." His brother started to laugh.

"You just found out you have a brother you never knew about and you're laughing? What kind of crazy family have I inherited?"

Taurean was silent for a moment.

"Mason, one of the things I've learnt since I've been here is that life is too short to worry about things that I have no control over. Yes, I can do all I want to try to confirm what you've said, but the truth is in the eyes. You have those Buchanan eyes. I noticed, but it wasn't anything strange since I've seen others with our eyes before. But it's only now you've told me that I've started to see the similarities. I hope you don't mind if I told my brothers. My mother may be another story, but I'm sure she'll come around."

Mason was unsure of what to say. He'd never expected Taurean's reaction to be like this.

"Tell me a bit about my brothers."

"You have two other brothers. Three if we count Corey. Patrick is the oldest…. Sorry." He smiled. "The second oldest. He's thirty-nine. He married and lives in Chicago. His wife is Paula, Alana's friend. Then there's Daniel. He too is married and has a son. He's almost one. He's the pastor of a church in Brooklyn. Our mom still lives in a small town outside Chicago called Oak Park."

"I can't wait to meet them." Mason tried to contain his excitement. If his other brothers were anything like Taurean, he was sure he'd like them.

Tonight had turned out better than he'd expected.

Now, all he had to deal with was this attraction to Lianne.

Chapter 8

Overhead the moon glowed, its fullness making Mason's way back to the resort easy. The night had turned out better than he'd imagined. He'd left the resort earlier in the evening wondering if he could tell his brother about his secret. Even while he'd sat at the dinner table, he had not been sure about what he should do.

Now, he felt better. His brother's reaction had definitely not been what he'd expected. Taurean had embraced him without hesitation. They'd talked for hours, filling in the blank stages of each other's life. Mason had felt Taurean's pain when he'd spoken about Corey, his younger brother, and the guilt he'd felt after he'd assisted his brother. But he knew his brother had finally come to terms with what he'd done.

Mason had learned a lot about his father—the man, the father and the priest. His father had been a strict man, and not often a fair one. He'd been a man whose self-righteousness had separated him from his son for seven years because of his unwillingness to forgive. Taurean had told Mason the story of his years in prison, and the "visit" to Barbados that had brought Alana and Melissa into his life.

Mason had learned about Alana and Melissa and all that had taken place almost two years ago when Alana's husband Blake Smith-Connell had tried to kill her. Mason could hear the intensity of Taurean's love for his wife and the little girl he now claimed as his own. He heard about the show in New York almost two years ago that had launched Alana's career. She was now one of the most talked-about new artists.

Taurean had looked a bit embarrassed when he'd showed Mason the picture that had made him famous. The picture, *The Birth of a Hero,* bore the strokes of love and he wondered if a woman would ever love him that way.

Now, with information he wanted to store in his

memories for further reflection, Lianne came to mind. He thought of the relationship between Taurean and his wife, and he felt an ache so intense he was stunned by its sharpness. He was tired of being alone, tired of the pace of a career that no longer satisfied him. But to dream of more with Lianne was like wishing for something that might never happen. She was definitely not the marrying kind.

She was most definitely not for him. She probably didn't want to get married either.

When Mason reached the path that lead to the resort, he turned toward an area of the grounds he'd never visited. The brochure called it the Flower Garden, a simple name, but a place where guests could relax surrounded by a potpourri of local flora and fauna.

As he neared the area, he noticed a figure ahead. Immediately, he knew who it was.

Lianne.

Where was she going?

When she turned in his direction, he moved swiftly into the shadow of the nearest tree. She stood still for a moment as if aware of his presence, but then she shook her head and continued on her way, meandering through the trees, but stopping briefly to look around herself.

For a while Mason could not see her, but when

she reappeared, he slipped behind a large boulder that decorated the most western side of the garden.

Instead of taking her exact route, he circled around the garden, reaching the boulder on the opposite side.

Like a cool night wind, voices whispered in the night. A lesser skilled person would have only heard the wind; instead, his years of experience helped him to separate the different sounds and he could almost hear their voices clearly.

He moved closer, at the same time noticing a large crack in the stony mass. When he slipped between the crack, he could hear the voices louder— clearer.

Lianne's voice was the first he heard. She'd lost the quiet gentility of her "station" and instead her voice was strong and direct.

"How's he doing? Sheila is worried about him."

"He's doing fine. Of course, he's more worried about them than himself. The case is going fine. He testifies in a few days and then it'll be all over."

"Over? Yes. But the price he's had to pay seems a bit too high. After this, they go directly into witness protection for the rest of their lives. How happy can they really be? No more contact with family. A change of life. It won't be easy."

"I understand, but what's happened to you? You've done this before and it's always been about getting the bad guy. I hope you're not getting soft on me."

"No, Brent, I'll be fine, but I can't help but feel what they're going through. Each time I hear a new report about the case, I can't help but be impressed with his courage."

There was a noise in the distance and he didn't hear the man's response. Then he heard Lianne again.

"Yes, at first he seemed so unassuming, but I've never come across someone who is more determined to do what is right. You can let Stan know that I'm fine. Damien is having the time of his life, but he still misses his father. I've been teaching him how to swim and he's picking up really fast. He can almost swim without much help."

"I'm glad things are as normal as they can be. Hopefully, this will soon be over."

There was a moment of silence.

"I need you to do something for me. I want you to run a check on a Mason Sinclair. He claims he's a FBI agent on leave. Get as much information on him as possible. And a picture. He seems legitimate, but I have to be sure."

There was silence again.

"So you have a beau."

Again, there was silence.

"I know I'm taking a risk but he seems fine and he provides additional cover. But yes, I'll be careful."

"Sounds a bit more than that to me. Don't let him break your heart, and make sure you don't lose focus. We don't want anything to go wrong."

"I know. I never lose focus."

"Good, keep it that way. It's almost ten o'clock. I have to go. I'll be here the same time on Saturday night."

"Good, I'm sure I'll have more news for you. Just be careful. We won't want to lose one of our best agents. You have the reputation of being the best."

Mason heard the sound of footsteps and then Lianne's anguished cry.

"What the hell have I got myself into? What am I going to do?"

Mason waited until he heard her footsteps before he crept around the other side of the boulder, his back pressed against it. He watched as Lianne walked away.

When he finally moved, there was no one in sight. Inside, anger like a boiling kettle bubbled. He felt betrayed. The Lianne he was slowly falling for didn't exist.

An agent? He'd suspected that something was wrong, but this…this…revelation went far beyond his speculations.

He strolled along the beach, his thoughts on what he'd just heard. He wasn't sure how to deal with it.

In the distance, he heard the bark of a dog—his dog. Maybe the dog would understand how he felt.

He knew he was being unreasonable. As an agent he should know better. She was only doing her job. She was right to be careful about his presence. He could be the person to take the family out. Already she'd shown a weakness by trusting him.

But he was proud of himself. His first impressions of her were correct. She wasn't a nanny by profession. She'd done a good job of playing the role. Only someone who knew what they were looking for would have seen the slight inconsistencies. And who said that a former agent couldn't have given up her job to be a nanny?

He wondered about the case she was working on. Who was the man? Sheila and Damien? From the conversation he'd heard, he knew that the husband was a witness in a serious case, and they would be going into witness protection when the case was over.

He knew he could make a few calls, but didn't think it would be a good idea. If he did any searching or asked too many questions, he could compromise the situation.

No, he'd find out eventually. Until then, he'd keep an eye on the beautiful Lianne Thomas.

Nanny?

Hell no!

Hearing scratching at his feet, he looked down and smiled when he saw Beach looking up at him.

"Come boy, you want to take a walk?" he said, bending slightly to stroke the dog's ears.

Beach nodded as if he understood every word. The dog then turned and took off down the beach at what seemed like a hundred miles an hour.

He stopped suddenly and turned, his tail wagging with excitement and a grin on his face.

"Okay, okay, I'm coming."

Maybe spending an hour or so with Beach would help Mason to clear his mind.

He definitely needed to come to grips with all that was happening.

Lianne watched as Mason walked along the beach, the dog, Beach, racing ahead and stopping to look back as if to tell him hurry. She laughed at the antics of the animal that had somehow become Mason's close friend. The unwavering trust the dog showed him suggested a lot about the man.

However, what had happened tonight had been a serious mistake. How could she have allowed someone to follow her? Ironically, the words that had been spoken to her at the same time Mason had been spying on her had been closer to the truth than she wanted to admit.

She didn't know how much he knew, but he'd

heard something. Of that she was sure. It had been only when she'd been walking away that she'd heard the slightest of noises. She'd continued to walk away, hiding in the shadows to see if someone would appear.

When Mason had stepped from behind the rock, she'd been angry at herself, but relieved that it was not someone else.

Mason knew. She didn't know how much he'd overheard, but she was sure he'd heard enough to draw conclusions.

She had two choices. She could either pretend that she didn't know or she could confront him about the situation.

As an agent, he should understand why she'd lied about her identity, but in situations like this, people were often irrational, only thinking of their feelings and the fact that they'd been lied to. Lianne hoped that Mason would deal with this in a mature way. She did not want to lose his friendship.

For the first time in a long time, she was actually intrigued by a man.

Mason represented all that she found appealing in a man. The strong silent type; handsome; sensitive; definitely a man. But like her, he carried secrets that could affect the nature of their relationship.

She kept asking herself why he was in Barbados,

and the reason he'd given, though reasonable, just didn't ring true.

One thing she had noticed was how he looked at Taurean when no one thought he was. The resemblance between the two of them was uncanny. There was a mystery there and she intended to find out the truth.

Mason Sinclair may be the man to capture her interest, but she had every intention of finding out what secret kept him here on the island.

Carolyn slowly came awake, blissfully content from the hours of lovemaking she'd spent. The dinner had been lovely. Garth had wined and dined her with the elegance of the gentleman he was. First, he'd taken her to a quaint and quiet restaurant on the outskirts of town, just on the lakeside. There, they'd dined on the night's special while listening to music from the early eighties—Earth, Wind and Fire, the Carpenters, Stevie Wonder, Olivia Newton-John and the Temptations. A pleasant mixture to satisfy the restaurant's mixed clientele.

She'd never intended on spending the night in Garth's bed. She'd left home with the firm resolve that she would be sleeping in her own bed. And she didn't. She was definitely in her own bed, but Garth had spent the whole night. There was no doubt

about what had happened. She remembered everything clearly. From the first tentative kiss to the
moment all hell had broken loose and she'd given
in to the burning need to feel Garth Wade lying
naked against her.

A need that had been well satisfied. Garth hadn't
left an inch of her body untouched. He'd taken her
to that special place where every color was more
vivid until the rainbow exploded, leaving her
basking in the afterglow of passion.

Her body ached, but it was a pleasant feeling.
Despite her pocketful of lovers, Garth had taken her
to a place only two men had taken her before.

Now, tears of sadness and joy flowed. She knew
that things would be different.

She was falling in love. Or was she already in
love? Carolyn glanced at the man who lay across
from her. She reached over to touch him, knowing
that he had to leave soon since he had an early class.

Garth did not respond, so she bent and kissed
him gently. This time he responded; his eyes flicked
open and he reached for her, kissing her with a desperation she did not expect.

He still wanted her.

She sighed with relief.

Their eyes met, lingered, and she saw the telltale
flicker of heat. She averted her eyes; she wanted to
look at him, but somehow she felt embarrassed.

She placed her head on his shoulder and wrapped her arms around him. She inhaled his musky scent.

Content with the physical contact, she untangled herself from around him and glanced at the clock on the dresser.

Nine-thirty.

A red Post-it note beckoned her. She slipped from between the sheets and quickly retrieved it.

Class at ten. Wake me up.

"Garth," she said, turning to face him, but realized he was already up.

"I know, I know," he replied. "I have a class at ten o'clock. No worry, I'll make it and since classes don't officially begin until ten minutes past the hour, I can make it easily." He rushed into the bathroom, his naked body stirring her with wanting.

Carolyn rushed downstairs. She would have a cup of coffee ready for him by the time he came down.

Ten minutes later, she watched as his car sped down the driveway.

Even now her body tingled from the kiss he'd given her just before he'd rushed through the door. A smile remained locked on her face, her memory of the night still vivid in her mind, her body's sensitivity evidence of the thorough attention he'd given to every inch of her.

Her body quivered with the memory of his touch.

Garth had been a sensitive, passionate lover. He'd not treated her with gentleness, taking her on several wild rides before he'd slowed the pace down and taken her to a place she'd not been to in recent times.

Again, she wondered if she was falling in love and knew she was treading on thin ice. She didn't want this. She wanted to be free to do whatever she wanted. She'd enjoyed her freedom and independence for too long to give it up so easily. Maybe they could just be lovers like all of the others and that would be enough. But she knew Garth. He was not like that and he would want more.

But she was too old to give her freedom up!

When John had passed away, she'd almost felt that her life would end, but slowly over time, she'd learned to survive and had basked in her singleness.

The first thing that crossed her mind was that she needed to call her son. She had not spoken to him in a while. Her anger at him for going to Barbados had finally abated. Now, she wondered if he'd told his brother, Taurean, the truth about his identity.

She really didn't want to think about this situation, especially after the night with Garth. She'd go to the country club and call Mason tonight.

She'd take a quick shower and then head on out to the country club to chair the meeting for the upcoming celebrity fashion show scheduled to take place two months away. Plans had been going well and she'd been instrumental in encouraging several up-and-coming African-American celebrities to attend. Last year, the organization had been thrilled when Oprah Winfrey had agreed to attend. They had raised over five million dollars to assist with the building of a children's wing at the local hospital. This year they hoped to establish a home for pregnant teens.

When Carolyn entered the shower a few minutes later, she'd completely put herself into get-ready-for-the-day mode, but thoughts of Garth still lingered in her mind and in the musky scent of the towel hanging on the rack. It was the subtle scent of maleness she loved.

Immediately, her body tingled and she closed her eyes, groaning with longing. Garth was taking over her mind and, for some reason after their night, the memory was not an unpleasant one. For the past few years she'd taken her dalliances with some intensity but they'd mostly been for amusement and she hoped that didn't make her a bad woman.

Carolyn turned the shower off, moving quickly to the bedroom. About to enter her walk-in closet, Carolyn was startled by the jarring cry of the phone.

Garth.

Her heart quickened.

"Good morning." She didn't know what else to say.

"Hi, did you sleep well? I'm sorry I had to go. I wanted nothing more than to make love to you this morning."

She did not respond; she could not breathe. The memory of all they'd done the night before still vivid in her mind.

"Carolyn, are you there?"

"Yes."

"Cat got your tongue?"

"No, I'm fine."

"Glad to know you are."

There was an uncomfortable pause.

"I hope you enjoyed last night. I did."

"I did, too. More than enjoyed it."

"I'm glad to know you did. Wouldn't have wanted to disappoint you."

"Of course you didn't."

"Wanna do it again sometime?" he teased.

"Yes, I'm open to any possibilities. Just make sure you're up to it. I don't tire easily."

He laughed. "Well, I'm willing to show you the stuff I'm made of. How'd you like to come to dinner tonight? At my home? I'll do the cooking."

"How can I refuse an invitation like that? I'll be sure to bring the dessert."

"Oh, I'll be looking forward to it."

"What time do you want me to be ready? Six?"

"Sounds good. I'll call a car service to pick you

up. I don't want you driving, since I intend to drive you home. Sorry, I won't be able to pick you up but I'll be in the kitchen."

"That's fine. I'm looking forward to tonight. Do you want me to bring a bottle of wine? Since you're doing the cooking, it's the least I can do."

"Definitely, bring a bottle of wine, but I already have something else in mind for dessert." His voice was low and husky. "Make sure you come prepared to eat. I'll see you later."

When the phone went silent, Carolyn realized that her mouth was wide open.

She was going to be the dessert.

The drive from Carolyn's home to Garth's took less than ten minutes. When the car turned into the gated driveway of a residence she'd passed often and admired, she could not help but be surprised. The house, partially hidden by the stately sassafras palms, had always sparked her curiosity.

The irony of the situation forced her to giggle. She was sure that the driver thought she was crazy, but the situation was truly hilarious.

When the car finally pulled up and she slipped out, she could not help but be amazed at the beauty and magnificence of the traditional colonial architecture. Surprisingly, the house's size did not detract from its elegant ambience.

Carolyn walked up the steps, waving at the driver as he pulled away. She felt as if she'd stepped into an earlier time. She could almost hear the voices of the original owners whispering in the trees.

When she reached the door, it automatically opened and a tiny woman stood there, a broad smile on her face.

"Welcome, Mrs. Sinclair. Garth is waiting for you. He told me to bring you straight to the kitchen. Follow me."

Carolyn followed the woman down a long hallway and then down a dimly lit corridor before she entered a massive doorway.

After thanking the woman, Carolyn entered the room. Garth had turned at the footsteps and now looked at her with a strange expression on his face.

"Carolyn, thanks for coming and welcome to my home."

"I'm glad I'm here. You have a lovely home."

"Thank you. I'm glad you like it. My parents died when I was in my late twenties and left this house for me. Most of what you see is what my mother would have done. I've made very few changes over the years."

"I'm glad you didn't make many changes. The house is beautiful as it is. I hope I can persuade you to give me a tour."

"Your wish is my command, Mrs. Sinclair. You

can take a seat. I'm soon done here. Just have to put the finishing touches and we're done."

Carolyn sat on one of the stools along the counter and watched as Garth quickly added lettuce and cucumber to the salad he was making. The speed at which he worked, she could tell that he was comfortable in the kitchen, unlike most of the men she knew. Even her late husband had never cooked. She didn't particularly like the domestic cap either, so cooking was a rarity in her home. Not that she couldn't do it; she just didn't like the task. Despite this, she'd made sure Mason knew his way around the kitchen.

When Garth was done, he wiped his hands and asked her to follow him. His hand rested against her elbow, giving her a warm, giddy feeling.

When they reached the sitting room, he picked up the phone and called Teresa to inform her they were ready to eat.

Teresa, the same woman who'd let her in, soon appeared, followed by another young woman, both carrying trays filled with food—the aroma of which sent Carolyn's taste buds into overdrive.

After the table was laid, the two women excused themselves.

"I'm definitely going to enjoy this meal," Carolyn said when they'd left. "Everything smells heavenly."

"Well, let's not waste any time."

An hour later, Carolyn wiped her mouth daintily and placed her dessert fork on the plate. She couldn't eat another bite of the cheesecake she'd agreed was the best she'd tasted anywhere. The experience could only be considered sinful.

Eating, however, was no longer on her mind. During the meal, she could not take her eyes off Garth. The meal had been more than just food. It had been a deliberate seduction of her senses, and ending with the cheesecake had been the ultimate climax.

"Come, I can't eat another bite. Let me pour each of us a glass of wine and we'll take that tour you wanted."

He rose and came to stand behind her. She could feel his heated body behind her and had the overwhelming desire to lean back. Instead, she stood, too, and said with a smile, "Lead the way. I'm in your hands."

His only response was a soft chuckle.

He led her down a corridor, up a flight of stairs and down another corridor when he stopped outside a door.

"We'll begin our tour here," he said, turning the knob and stepping back for her to enter.

She stepped in and a cry of surprise escaped her lips. ·

"I didn't expect us to start the tour here, but it is the perfect place to start."

Realizing that she was giving her approval, Garth closed the door and pulled her to him.

"Woman, I've waited so long to hold you in my arms."

Her only reply was a groan of contentment.

When his lips touched hers, Carolyn knew she'd found what she'd been searching for all those years since John's death.

She parted her lips, closed her eyes, and enjoyed the taste of the man who'd captured her heart…and soul.

Chapter 9

The sun had risen in all its splendor, a sight that Lianne had grown accustomed to in the past few weeks. The kiss she'd exchanged with Mason the night before had affected her more than she wanted. Already, the midday sun had brought with it blistering heat. Fortunately, the cool winds of the Atlantic Ocean provided the much needed relief.

Today she didn't feel like going into the water. Sheila and Damien had decided to remain indoors, borrowing several DVDs from the small library provided for the guests. Carolyn had decided to remain in her room. She wondered what Mason was doing; wondered if he was thinking about her as she did about him. She hated this feeling of helplessness that came with the attraction to a male. She always felt as if she were giving a part of herself over; that she was losing who she was. Maybe she was doing the wrong thing by allowing herself to fall for Mason. And she was on the job. Stan was adamant about no involvements on the job, but fighting an attraction to a man like Mason was more difficult than she'd thought.

Last night, for the first time in her life, she'd dreamed of a happily-ever-after. Sometime during the night she'd awoke, stunned by the dream that she'd had. She'd seen herself in a white wedding dress, the handsome Mason smiling at her before his lips covered hers, drinking from what she willingly offered. She had also seen him on the sand, tumbling around with two little boys with brandy-colored eyes.

Maybe, she was going crazy. Maybe she was falling in love.

She giggled nervously.

In love?

No, she couldn't be. She didn't know him well enough, but there was a measure of truth in the thought. There was just something about Mason Sinclair that was so appealing.

It was the smile, but it was so much more. It was

the way he struggled when she knew he was in pain. It was his gentle smile and the way he communicated with a cautious, homeless dog.

Lianne moved quickly over to the phone. She was going to do something she shouldn't, but she needed to see him. She dialed the number to reception, asking for his room number, and the operator automatically transferred her. He picked the phone up on the second ring, his voice controlled, seeming puzzled.

"Hello."

"May I speak to Mason?"

"Speaking." She heard a change in his voice.

"This is Lianne. I was wondering what you're doing tonight. Sheila and Damien are attending a party for the kids this evening, so I'm free. How'd you like to go to dinner at the restaurant with me?"

For a moment, he didn't say anything. She could almost hear his surprise.

"Thanks," he eventually replied, "I'd love to go to dinner with you."

"Would an hour from now be okay?"

"Yes, perfect. Where do I meet you?"

"In the lobby."

"I'll be there. Thanks for the invitation."

"Bye," she said before she replaced the phone.

For a while she stared at the phone wondering if she'd done the right thing. It was too late to think of that anyway. She'd already committed to an evening with him.

She turned from the phone and immediately wondered what to wear. She'd not brought anything formal, but she thought of the close-fitting ivory dress she'd brought in case she needed something a bit less casual.

She hadn't worn it before, having only bought it in England when she'd been there during the summer. Her mother had insisted she bring something besides the pants she loved to wear. Not that she didn't like dresses, nor being feminine, but it wasn't often the opportunity arose to dress up. However, tonight she wanted Mason to see her as a woman and not the agent she was.

Mason looked at himself one final time in the mirror and walked from the bathroom. He searched for his cane, eventually finding it just by the door. Reaching it, he picked it up, opened the door and closed it behind him. As he walked along the corridor to the elevator, he wondered if he wasn't too overdressed. He'd spent more time than usual choosing his clothes and getting ready.

The white cotton shirt fitted him snugly, emphasizing his toned chest, his broad shoulders and the firm ripple of his six-pack. Despite his bum leg, his body had maintained much of its form. Yes, he'd lost weight, but it only served to give him a leaner more predatory look.

The khaki trousers, though loose-fitting, emphasized the muscles of his legs. Mason knew he looked good. He'd been with enough women and knew how they responded to him. His slight limp annoyed him, but he'd realized since being on the island that most women saw this as a vulnerability and wanted to comfort him.

The elevator opened and he stepped out, his gaze immediately landing on Lianne. His heart stopped.

Damn, she was fine. He'd never seen a more beautiful woman. Not the artificial kind of beauty that women paid thousands of dollars to achieve, but the unassuming gentle kind of beauty that the woman herself didn't recognize.

And Lianne was definitely that kind of woman.

Her eyes widened when she saw him, and her head bowed as if she didn't want him to see the flash of desire. When she looked up, her strength and confidence slammed him full in the chest and he knew her moment of weakness had passed.

But her erect stance and the straightened back made him realize she was affected by his presence.

"You look even more beautiful tonight. I'll be the envy of the men in the restaurant."

"Thank you and so do you. I'm sure the women

will want to tear my hair out." He heard the laughter in her voice.

"Well, you have nothing to worry about there. I intend to give all my attention to the prettiest lady in the restaurant." For a moment he stared at her. "So, are you ready to go? Sorry, I can't take your hand, but the cane is a bit of an inconvenience."

"Mason, it's not a problem. I understand."

They turned to walk toward the resort's indoor restaurant.

When they reached the entrance, the rolling sound of steel-pan music welcomed them. At the entrance, the hostess greeted them and quickly directed them to their seats. He pulled Lianne's chair out before lowering himself in the chair opposite.

"So what's your pleasure?" he asked.

"Shouldn't I be the one to ask that question since I invited you to dinner?"

He smiled, a slow mischievous look, before he answered. "Sorry, my mother always reminds me that I must be a gentleman in every situation, so call it force of habit. I bow to your wishes, my lady."

"Mason, I'm only kidding. I would, however, like to ask your recommendation since I know you've eaten here often."

"I have? And what little birdie told you that?"

"No birdie. Just a matter of deduction. I know

you don't eat at the outside restaurant, so it would have to be here."

"Brilliant, Watson. Wonderful process of deduction. However, that's not the issue of tonight. I'll be the perfect gentleman and order for you."

He glanced at the menu, aware of her lingering gaze.

"I'm going to recommend the Island Delight."

"What's that?"

"Several local flying fish steamed in a spicy Creole sauce served with local vegetables and either rice or grilled parsley potatoes. I've tried it before and it's one of the best dishes on the menu."

"It sounds great. I can't wait. I'm definitely feeling hungry. I tried not to eat too large a meal today."

The dinner had been great and the conversation better. Now, the white brilliance of the moon's rays cast gentle shadows across the beach. In the distance, Lianne could hear the waves lash against the shore.

Her body tingled with anticipation. She knew that she wanted Mason to kiss her and knew that before the night was over, he'd oblige her. She'd seen it in every glance, every touch. Strangely enough, she'd realized that Mason Sinclair was a toucher.

As they walked, he held her hand and she hoped he didn't feel her tremble, but a firm squeeze made her realize he was aware of the effect of his touch.

And then he stopped and turned to her, drawing her to him. She'd wondered for days if her reaction would be the same as before. All that she expected and wished for didn't come close to what she experienced.

This time, she'd expected shooting stars and the brilliant flash of lightning, but neither came.

Instead she felt the whisper of the wind against her lips and when his lips touched hers, there was the spark of a flame inside that slowly began to burn. Not the painful heat, but something hot that brought pleasure. She tried to close her eyes but realized they already were.

And then he groaned and she almost came undone when she felt his hand cup her behind and draw her close to him. She pressed herself even closer, enjoying the warmth and thickness of his arousal.

He was huge.

She moved back slightly, placing a hand between them until she felt his heat and the surge of pulsating blood.

She felt his body shiver and his mouth moved from hers. She wanted to scream *No,* but he spoke before she could.

"If you don't want me to embarrass myself tonight, you're going to have to keep your hands to yourself. I only have a certain measure of control. And I'm sure neither of us is ready for what a whole night may demand of us."

"Ok, but don't talk, just kiss me."

Mason was willing to oblige. He'd always known that she would be passionate. She did everything with intensity. She parted her lips, this time allowing him to taste her very essence.

But he wanted to taste more of her, wanted to feel his lips again the firm round breasts that peaked against his chest.

He took his hand and cupped the first breast, loving the feel of her in his hands. He reached for the zip at her back, expertly lowering it. She wore no bra and for a while he just stared as they pointed their arousal at him.

The moonlight caressed them making them seem magical, but he knew what he saw was very real. He lowered his lead, taking one firm nipple between his lips while his hand caressed the other.

"God, I'm burning inside. Mason, you're going to have to stop or I'm going to want to go to your room tonight and I can't do that," she moaned.

"Lianne, you're an amazing woman," Mason said, his mouth trailing upward until his lips hovered over hers. "Most people wouldn't realize there was so much passion, but I knew from the time I saw you that a warm, passionate woman lay beneath."

As if to confirm what he said, Lianne groaned, arching herself against him.

"I want to make love to you so bad. But I agree

it's not the right time. But I can promise you that this won't end here. I've not felt this way about a woman for years, but there's something about you that makes me feel like a randy teenager."

He stopped talking to straighten her dress.

"Come sit here with me awhile. Let's enjoy the island's moonlight."

He led her to the nearby chair, sat and then lowered her onto his lap, wrapping his arms around her.

Together they looked out across the ocean. It was at this time that the island was at its most beautiful. White moonbeams caressed the now quiet sea, its mood contrasting with its restless energy during the day.

There was a slight scuffle in the sand, and Beach appeared out of the darkness.

"How's it, boy?"

The dog whimpered. He drew closer, resting his head against Mason's shoe. He looked up, noticing Lianne, but decided to ignore her.

For a while they sat there, Mason aware of Lianne on his lap, his hands rubbing her back.

"Come, it's time that we go. It's getting late."

Lianne jumped up. "I'm so sorry, I forgot about your leg. I hope I didn't…"

"No, something else may be hurting, but it's definitely not my leg," he replied.

He rose slowly from where he sat, stretching

each leg to ease the stiffness out. No, he was fine. Her weight had not done any permanent damage.

He took her hand in his and led her toward the resort. They walked in silence and it was only when they reached her door that she turned before she entered and looked up at him.

"I just wanted to say thank you for accepting my invitation to dinner. I had a great night."

He couldn't answer, all he could focus on were her swollen, trembling lips. He wanted to kiss her again.

He lowered his head and immediately she responded to him.

When he pulled away he saw the desire in her eyes. He only had to say the word and he'd be in her room tearing her clothes off.

"And thank you for the invitation. The pleasure was all mine. I hope we can do it again soon."

She turned from him, unlocked the door and disappeared inside without looking back.

And then he did the strangest thing. He pressed his palms against the door, as if wanting to feel her warmth.

He was going all crazy and romantic.

Definitely not what he was looking for! His life was too much in shambles and limbo.

Lianne closed the door behind herself, immediately placing her back against it. Mason Sinclair was an enigma. He was doing things to her that she didn't want. He was everything she wanted.

She was falling in love with him.

There, she'd finally said it.

In the few weeks she'd known him, she'd acknowledged the attraction, but tonight, she realized that all she'd admired about him was what made him so noble and unique.

Lianne moved over to the bed, slipping her shoes off and lying on her back, her eyes taking in the wide expanse of ceiling.

She wasn't sure what to do about the realization, but she knew she didn't want a relationship. That would mean giving up the independence that had become so much a part of her life. Yes, she wanted to make love to him and she knew that once would not be enough, but she'd be on the island for the next week or two and that would be enough time to enjoy each other's company…and bodies.

Though marriage was rarely on her mind, she wanted to be happy and, yes, she wanted marriage. But she didn't want it now. She had too many plans for her career and they didn't involve being in a relationship or getting married.

So where did she go from here? First up, she needed to be honest with Mason, tell him the truth about her assignment, though he already knew most of what was going on. She was breaking all the rules in her personal rule book, but she'd made the decision and she'd have to live with it.

She picked up the phone on the tiny desk that was always found in a hotel room, dialed the hotel reception and asked for Mason's room.

He picked up the phone on the first ring.

"Mason, this is Lianne. I need to talk to you about something important. Are you already in bed?"

"No, I'm just watching television."

"Can you come over to my room, I need to talk to you."

"Okay, I'll be over in a bit. Just need to get some clothes on."

Lianne was not sure she liked the image that flashed immediately in her mind, so she willed it away and said, "Good, I'll be waiting for you."

When he knocked on the door several minutes later, Lianne immediately opened it.

"Come," she said, "let's sit on the balcony."

He followed her, and when she gestured for him to sit, he complied.

"Lianne, relax, you're usually so controlled. What's the matter?"

"I haven't been totally honest with you. But as you know, it makes no sense me hiding my identity. I'm aware of your detective work the other night."

"Detective work?"

"Yes, I know you were there when I spoke to my partner the other night on the beach."

"You saw me. I must be losing my skill. I don't make mistakes like that."

"Nothing to worry too much about. It was just the slightest of noises. Most people won't have heard it."

"Well, I guess you're better than most at your job?"

"So I've been told."

"Hell, I'm sorry, I didn't really mean to spy, but curiosity got the better of me. I noticed a few inconsistencies over the time I've known you, so when I saw you the other night, heading out to the Flower Garden, I knew something was up. I'm an agent, I couldn't help it. So you're really not a nanny?"

"No, I'm definitely not a nanny. Since you overheard my conversation with my partner, it really didn't make sense hiding the reason for my...*our* being here. Another pair of eyes would be help."

"No, Lianne. I can't go back to that kind of work. It'll only send me crazy. When I came out of hospital, I wanted nothing to do with the Bureau anymore. I just wanted to put my partner's death behind me and move on. I haven't changed my mind."

"I understand. There are several other agents at the resort, so I'm sure we'll be fine, and there's no indication that Cordoni knows anything."

"Cordoni? I know that name."

"I'm sure you've heard it. About two years ago, he killed one of his partners, and one of his employees, Jason Clarkson, witnessed the whole thing and decided that the right thing to do was testify."

"I remember now. Cordoni is one of the largest crime bosses in New York. The man he killed was McMaster, right?"

"Yes, that's the case."

"I remember thinking that the witness must be either a really stupid man, or very brave. Situations like this are never easy for the witness."

"Yes, Clarkson is an incredible man. Several attempts were made to try to find out his whereabouts. I'm assuming that after that, mail threats were made on the wife and child's lives, so Clarkson gave us an ultimatum. Protect his wife or he won't testify."

"He gave them an ultimatum? He must have known how important getting Cordoni is."

"True, he did. So an agreement was made and I was one of the agents to come to the island. My partner is also here. He's the one I was talking to last night."

"So it means everything is all right for now, so my help is not needed. There's not much I could have done anyway with my leg in this condition."

"Thanks for understanding. I know that you

found out because of a mistake I made, but if I could have told you earlier, I would have."

"Lianne, no worry, you should know that I knew the importance of the confidentiality. Suppose I were the one coming after Sheila and Damien?"

"True, but I know you aren't. Sometimes, one has to go with instinct, that gut feeling, and mine tells me you're all right."

"I'm going to leave you for the night, but we'll talk more about this in the morning."

The man closed the door behind himself and immediately moved toward the phone. He quickly dialed the familiar number. His contact answered it on the second ring. "I have some news for you," he said. "I know where they are. They are on the island of Barbados."

"Barbados? The Caribbean island? You're quicker than I thought. When do you leave?"

"I couldn't get on a flight tomorrow, but I'm booked for the next day. I have some stuff I need to take care of first."

"But I want her dead today, not tomorrow."

"Clarkson doesn't testify until next week. I'm sure his testimony is being kept for the last. It'll have the greatest impact, especially after all the boring scientific information. I'll make sure the deed is done. These things make for proper planning. And I have no intention of leaving any evidence that can trace things to either of us. I'm a professional."

"Well, take your time. As long as you get the job done. I'll deposit the first half of the fee to the account, you've earned it, and the rest when the job is complete."

"As I've said from the beginning, I always get the job done. I'll contact you in a few days."

The man listened to the click before he moved to the room where his younger brother sat waiting. They'd both decided their brother wouldn't go to jail and they were going to do anything in their power to ensure he didn't. He'd already been in prison for almost one year and it was time Clarkson paid for his betrayal. The man had surprised them. They'd never expected him to turn down the offer of money, so he had to die. It'd proven harder than they had expected, but it had been only a matter of time before they'd found them. He'd let Shark take care of the woman and child. There was nothing he wouldn't do to ensure that this happened.

Chapter 10

A few days later, Lianne sat with Sheila on the balcony overlooking the beach. The past few days had been difficult for both of them. Damien had taken ill, running a high fever, and she'd helped Sheila watch over him. She had not slept much in that time. Today was the first day they had really been able to relax. Damien's fever had finally broken and now he was resting quietly. The first thing he'd asked when he'd finally woken up was if he could go to the beach.

Sheila had promised she'd carry him along the beach in a few days, but he wouldn't be able to go into the water.

Lianne had only caught a glimpse of Mason on the few days she'd been confined to the room. She'd watched as he'd walked on the beach, his niece holding his hand as they walked. Sometimes, at unexpected moments, she would hear his laughter, but most times, what she heard was the delightful sound of Melissa. Sometimes, they'd be joined by twin girls. Lianne knew immediately that they were Melissa's best friends. She'd heard enough about Karen and Kerry from Melissa and Damien.

She was glad, however, that she'd told Mason the truth about her stay in Barbados. The burden she'd carried around had proven to be too heavy to bear. Telling him the truth had given her a sense of relief.

She picked up her cell phone and dialed the number of the Bureau. She needed to tell Stan what she'd done.

The phone rang for a while before he answered.

"Hello." As expected, his gruff voice came across the ocean.

"Stan, it's Lianne."

"You finally decided to give me a call. At least you've been reporting to Monroe, but I would have liked to speak to you too."

"Is that an indication that you miss me, Stan?"

"Miss you, my ass. I don't miss anyone. I'd just like you to come back here and get to the pile of cases that will soon be placed on your desk."

"Stan, you know I'll soon be home. Isn't Clarkson scheduled to testify in the next few days?"

"Yes and once he has, you'll be coming back here. So how are Sheila and the boy doing?"

"Under the circumstances, they're holding up better than I thought. I think being here on the island has helped them not think of him all the time. Damien loves the sea and if Sheila allowed it, he'd be in the water all day."

"Good, I'm glad to hear. And how are you holding up?"

"I'm holding up fine. It's not often I get paid to spend time on one of the most beautiful holiday islands in the world."

"Come on, come on, Lianne. You're tempting me. Makes me want to get my wife, pack my bags and head on down to Barbados."

"Maybe you should, Stan. You haven't taken a holiday in ages. I'm sure that Audrey would be delighted if you took some time off."

"To be honest, Lianne, I've been thinking more and more about that. I'm old enough to put in my papers and have enough to take care of Audrey and me for the rest of our lives. She's due for retirement, too, so we've been giving it some serious thought."

"Stan, I'm glad to hear. I'd be sorry to see you go, but I'm sure you would prefer to spend some quality time with Audrey now, you're…time is catching up with you."

"You trying to tell me I'm getting old?"

"Who, me? Stan, you know I'd never do that."

"So what have you called me about? It had to be something important for you to call."

"I've run into a situation of my own making. I made a mistake and I just wanted to tell you about it."

"Go ahead."

"There's an agent with the FBI who's on the island recuperating from being shot in the line of duty. His partner died in the shootout. The other night when I met Brent for my update, neither of us saw him following us, and he overheard most of what we talked about. Of course, when he saw me sneaking in to the garden, he followed. I didn't realize he was there until Brent left and I was about to leave when I heard a slight noise, but I pretended not to hear. He eventually came from behind a boulder close to where we were chatting."

"Who is he?"

"His name is Mason Sinclair and he works out of D.C. I asked Brent to find out as much about him as possible, but nothing inconsistent has turned up."

"I should be annoyed, but since he's an agent everything should be okay. I'll check out his supervisor and see if we have anything to worry about. How do you feel about him?"

"My gut feeling tells me he's the real deal, but I'm not perfect. I like him, so I don't want to be clouded by judgment backed on feelings."

"Lianne, I've seen how your gut feelings work, and you've never made any mistakes. I'm sure he'll turn out to be okay."

"I hope so, too."

"So do I hear a bit more than just *like?* It's about time you find yourself a good man and get married."

"That'll be telling, but yes, I really like him."

"Good, at least you'll have something after this is all over. You're like a daughter to me and I want to see you settled. For now, your job may seem like the only thing you need, but a job can never keep you warm at nights. I have to go. My secretary tells me that the Chief is on my other line. You take care. We'll talk again soon."

Lianne put the phone down and stared into the distance. What Stan had said was so true. She was devoted to her job, but when the nights were cold and she lay in bed alone, she ached for a warm body next to hers.

More and more these days she was becoming aware of her loneliness. Fortunately, her attraction to Mason was more than that. It was not just a simple need to have someone. It went much further.

Her attraction to him had been like the sudden

eruption of a long dormant volcano. She didn't only want him to take away some of the loneliness she felt; she wanted to know him in the most profound and intimate way possible. She wanted a glimpse into his heart and soul and body.

She'd always said that if she were to ever find herself in a serious relationship, it was would be one based on all the qualities she didn't see in her parents' marriage.

Maybe, she could find that someone in Mason.

Mason picked up the phone. He needed to call Lianne.

For the past few days he'd missed her. So when he'd discovered that Damien was ill, he knew it'd be a while before she'd be able to spend time with him.

However, when he'd returned from breakfast, she'd left a message on the answering machine in his room asking him to call her.

He took his time, not wanting to sound too anxious to hear her voice. Steadying his breathing, he punched in the number for her room and waited.

"Hello." Her voice was like summer rain after a long drought. He tried to calm the rapid beat of his heart.

"Hi, Lianne, you asked me to call."

"Hi, Mason. I'm so sorry, I didn't get a chance to call. Damien has not been well and we've been rotating the times to take care of him. Yesterday the fever broke and we were able to rest all afternoon and night."

"I did hear from the resort messenger, Melissa, that Damien was really ill."

Lianne laughed. "I'm sure that one day Melissa will take over the running of the resort. She knows everything that's important at the hotel."

"Yes, my niece is a pint-size Lois Lane."

"Your niece?"

"Yes, Taureon is actually my brother. I'll have to fill you in on the details later."

"I should have guessed. The resemblance between you two is uncanny. I can't wait for the story."

"Well, the reason I called was to ask you how you'd like to come with me to one of the most beautiful places on the island tomorrow. Sheila is getting a break while I take Damien today. Tomorrow, I have the day off and my partner will be spending some time with them on the beach. I need to get away from the hotel for a while."

"Of course, I'll go with you. I've been cramped up at the hotel for too long and definitely need to see some of the island. When do you want me to be ready?"

"Oh, we can leave in the morning. I've been to both places before, so I won't have any problems finding them."

"Good, I'll definitely be ready to go."

"Thanks, Mason. I have to go. Damien is calling me. Since he's feeling much better all he's been doing is eating. I ordered a pizza for him this morning and it's almost gone."

"Bye, you take care. I'll see you in the morning."

Mason strolled to the bed after he'd put the phone down. Good, she wanted to spend some time with him. And the feeling was mutual.

He'd definitely missed seeing her in the past few days, so their little outing was welcome. He enjoyed spending time with Lianne and this was the perfect opportunity to be with her.

He sprawled on the bed, his eyes closed.

Yes, he couldn't wait until tomorrow.

The next morning, Lianne moved slowly down the stairs. The elevator was taking too long to come and she really didn't want to delay further, knowing that Mason would be waiting for her in the lobby. She had her map, the basket of food she'd had the resort prepare for them and she was looking forward to a bright sunny day.

When she reached the lobby, she scanned the area, but did not see him. About to go to the receptionist to call his room, she noticed that he had arrived and was chatting with a woman.

Lianne stopped in her tracks as the woman

placed her hand on his shoulder, drawing him nearer. What was she planning to do? Kiss him?

Over her dead body.

Determined to stop this, she moved swiftly toward Mason and the woman.

Mason noticed her as she started walking and touched the woman on her shoulder, then started toward Lianne.

When they were standing before each other, Lianne said, "I can see you're already having a great day."

He didn't say anything at first, but then a broad grin spread on his face.

"Well, I do declare, Ms. Thomas, that you're jealous."

"Jealous? Me? Why should I be jealous?"

"Oh, well, if you're not jealous, I'll eat that whole basket of food. But it does feel good to know you care."

"Come, let's go before you say something you shouldn't," she teased.

Several minutes later, they were cruising along the road heading toward Harrison's Cave in the parish of St. Thomas.

While they drove they talked about cases they'd worked on and the satisfaction that both got from solving a case and bringing criminals to justice.

On the radio, the youthful voice of Barbadian

singing sensation Rihanna provided a perfect addition to the jovial mood they were both feeling.

When Lianne turned into the driveway of Harrison's Cave, she noticed the parking lot was almost full. Though mention of the cave had been made in travel documents as early as the eighteenth century, it was only in 1970 when the government had hired a speleologist to map the cave that the potential as a tourist attraction had been realized.

After paying the admission fee, they stood along with other tourists awaiting one of the many trams that took them on the spectacular ride into the heart of the cave.

Several minutes later, seated at the back of the tram with Mason, Lianne could not help but be amazed by the marvel of nature.

The cave was simply phenomenal. Though much of its color was enhanced by artificial lighting, this did not diminish the natural beauty. With shimmering stalagmites and stalactites, the kaleidoscope of colors only served to create an almost magical place. Crystal-clear pools of water revealed tiny fish that had somehow found their way to a home that was not quite real.

One of the most breathtaking moments of the tour was when the tram stopped and they were allowed to disembark and observe a majestic waterfall.

When the tram finally drove out of the cave, Mason knew he had experienced something truly awesome. He'd seen the work of God's hands in nature before, but Harrison's Cave rivaled many of those in larger metropolitan countries.

"I don't have to ask if you enjoyed the tour," Lianne commented as they drove out of the parking lot. "I've been a few times and the experience always leaves me breathless."

"I can see why. I don't believe I've ever seen something so beautiful."

"Me, too. And I've done some traveling, but this has been one of the most moving experiences."

As they drove away from Harrison's Cave, they both realized they'd experienced something important. They'd caught a glimpse of the wonderful power of the Creator.

Carolyn watched as Garth walked slowly toward her. When he called her this morning and asked her to meet him in the park, she'd wondered why, but he had not said, only indicating he wanted to speak to her about something important.

Now, as the sun, hidden behind the trees, prepared to take its nightly rest, she watched him move toward her. Though his walk appeared leisurely, his unsmiling face gave evidence of his purpose.

When he reached her, Garth bent his head, capturing her lips in a warm kiss. All day, she'd dreaded the worst. He wanted to break up with her, but the kiss confused her. This was not what she'd expected.

Maybe he just wanted one last kiss.

When he moved his lips away, she felt empty, but anger built inside. How could he want to break it off and still come here trying to make love to her?

Garth lowered himself onto the bench.

"I'm sorry I'm a bit late, but one of my graduate students came to my office as I was leaving and delayed me a bit. I hope you didn't think I'd stood you up," he said.

"I really wasn't sure what to think," she mumbled.

When he looked at her, his eyes seemed softer, tender. "Carolyn, why did you think I called you here?"

She didn't answer. Maybe she was being a fool.

"I don't believe you could think that I would call you here to break up with you." His tone served to reprimand her. "Do you think so little about my feelings for you?"

Again she was at a loss for words.

"I wanted to come here because it was the first place we met. I wanted this to be special."

Carolyn's heart began to race. She still wasn't sure what he wanted to say, but at least she knew it wasn't bad. Maybe he wanted to get serious, and exclusively date her.

"I asked you to come here because I wanted to ask you something serious."

"Yes, what's it?" she asked.

"I want you to marry me." He waited for her reaction and when she started to laugh, his eyes widened.

"I did expect a reaction, but I assure you that was not the one I expected. I thought it'd be a simple yes or no."

"I'm sorry. I really thought you'd called me here to break up."

"Break up? Why would you think so? Have I ever given you cause to think that I didn't enjoy your company? Didn't care about you?"

"No, you haven't and I'm sorry. I did not mean to hurt you. I was being silly by jumping to conclusions."

"Not hurt, disappointed."

"Then I'd have to say yes."

"I was about to say you have no choice, but you'll probably refuse me now. So what do you say? Think you'd want to marry a younger man that loves you more than life itself?"

Carolyn gasped. She was sure she'd not heard him correctly. "You love me?"

"Yes, did you ever doubt it?"

She didn't answer at first, but when she did, there was shock in her eyes.

But when she dared to look at him, she saw all that he'd said pooled there.

He did love her.

"I love you, too."

As the words slipped from her lips, he leaned toward her, capturing her mouth. She tasted him, enjoying the feel of him against her.

Somehow she knew everything was going to be all right.

When he pulled away, she felt that familiar emptiness. She'd not felt this way in years; that intense sense of oneness with another individual.

Resting against the bench, Garth placed his arms around her.

Carolyn watched as darkness fell, and the park lights slowly flickered on.

"So are you going to marry me, Ms. Carolyn Sinclair?"

"Yes, Mr. Wade."

Carolyn listened to the music of her heart. Somehow God had seen fit to send love into her life again.

Mason watched as Lianne, Alana and Sheila walked toward the beach. Damien, a distance ahead, skipped and flipped somersaults, causing the adults to break out in laughter.

And then something caught Mason's attention.

Something was wrong. A sudden movement in the shadows. The man, his eyes focused on Sheila, seemed out of place in the midst of casually clad tourists. He wore black and moved with the agility of a predator.

Mason turned, his own movement too sudden, causing him to stumble. His cane rolled down the steps. He moved as quickly as he could, the pain racing up his leg, but he knew time would not wait. He reached the bottom of the steps and bent to grab his cane. Moving as quickly as he could, he watched the man slither closer to the three who were still unaware of the impending danger.

The man was a real amateur, keeping his eyes on his intended victims and not looking back. If he had been vigilant he would have noticed Mason behind him.

Mason watched as the man reached into his pocket and knew instinctively that he had a gun. The telltale flash of sunlight against metal confirmed his suspicions.

Mason tried to speed up, but the pain in his leg had intensified. When the man unexpectedly looked back, Mason deliberately dropped his cane and then bent to retrieve it.

As he straightened, the man reached into his jacket, withdrew the gun and aimed.

With lightning speed, Mason hurled the cane in

the man's direction, striking his hand. A loud bang burst out and then the gun sailed through the air.

Chaos ensued, and Mason noticed that Lianne immediately sprang into action. The man realized it was impossible to find his gun, turned around and headed in Mason's direction. Seeing Mason, he swerved but then swung back, deliberately slamming into Mason and knocking him to the ground before he disappeared into the stampeding crowd.

As Mason tried to lift himself from the ground, Lianne sprinted by. Each time he tried to stand, another person slammed into him.

All he could hear were the echoes of screaming people around him. A hand reached out to him and he looked up.

Taurean.

"Are you all right, bro?"

"Yes. Go check on Sheila Clarkson and her son. I need to know if they're all right. Lianne? Where is she?"

"She's gone after the shooter. Come, you need to sit over there. Your leg's okay?"

"It's hurting like hell, but I'll be fine."

"Stay here until I get your cane and then I'm going to go find out what the hell is going on here."

Taurean retrieved the cane, handed it to his brother and then turned and walked to where Sheila and Damien sat surrounded by two men holding weapons.

When Mason stood to his feet, a sharp pain surged through his leg, but it slowly subsided until it was a dull ache. He needed to talk to Sheila.

When he reached her, he realized Damien was crying and Sheila was trying to calm him. Her cheeks were streaked with tears. Taurean was talking to one of the men.

"Are you all right?" Mason asked when she looked up and saw him.

"I'm okay. Scared Damien a bit but he'll be all right."

Mason could see that her body shook and he knew she was afraid. "They've found us. My God, they've found us. We're going to have to leave," she cried.

When she realized she'd said too much, she looked at him, a look of immediate mistrust, and then she smiled.

"Sorry, Mason, I'm so confused. Lianne told me you were an agent and that she told you about our situation."

"Yes, you're safe with me. When Lianne comes back, she's going to have to make a call. I'm sure she'll catch the man."

For a while he sat with them. Soon, Damien stopped crying and Mason tried all he could to make him smile.

"Lianne, Lianne!" Damien shouted.

Immediately, Mason stood. When Lianne reached them, he asked, "Did you catch him?"

"No, he got away." He heard her anger and frustration. "A car was waiting for him. There were no license plates so I'm not even sure if a trace will help. Can you take Sheila and Damien to their suite? I'm going to have to chat with the local police and find out what we're going to do. One of the agents and my partner are in your brother's office. They're calling Washington. I'll come up to the room as soon as I'm done here."

With that she turned and walked away, her stride long and purposeful.

She seemed a different person. Stronger, in control. Mason found this Lianne fascinating.

"Come," he said to Damien and his mother. "Let's go."

Half an hour later, there was a knock on the door. Cautiously, he peered through the peephole.

Melissa.

Mason opened the door and she stepped inside, holding a bag in her hand.

"Hello, Uncle Mason. I asked my dad if I could come over and bring some ice cream and cookies for Damien. I was on my way to the beach when the crazy man started shooting and I heard Damien was crying."

He felt a surge of pride. Each member of his

family was turning out to be what he'd hoped. Melissa's concern for her young friend was endearing. Damn, he was so proud.

"You can hug me if you want."

He smiled, lowered his head and hugged her.

"I'm glad you're my uncle."

"Thanks, I couldn't want a nicer niece. Come, let's go give Damien his ice cream. I'm sure you'd love some, too."

Sheila and Damien were sitting on the bed watching television, both laughing at the antics of the loveable Scooby-Doo.

Sheila took the ice cream and went into the small kitchenette. She soon returned with ice cream for each of them.

When the cartoon was over, a raucous game of charade kept Mason laughing until tears trickled down his cheeks. He was sprawled on the ground, his hearty laughter filling the room when the door opened and Lianne walked in.

And that's how Lianne found Mason when she entered the room. His laughter stopped her in her tracks. This was a Mason she hadn't yet encountered. He'd always seemed so serious and intense. She knew the reason for his personality and mood. He'd been through so much in the past few months—the discovery of his real father, the meeting with his brother, the death of his partner. So, seeing him laughing and animated forced her to see him in a different light.

On seeing her, Damien jumped up and squealed. "Lianne, Lianne. I thought you'd never come back. I hope you caught the bad man. Want some ice cream? Melissa brought us some maple-almond and the one with marshmallows. I can't remember the name."

"I'd love some ice cream, but give me a while. I want to talk to your mom and Mason about some adult business, but as soon as we're done, we'll continue playing charades. I'll even order pizza from the restaurant. Melissa, you'll take care of him for us?"

"Oh, course, I've babysat before, so I'm sure I can. And Damien is my friend."

When Melissa and Damien left the room, Lianne gave Mason and Sheila a rundown of all she'd found out from the police and the two agents. Agent Smart had almost lost his life, but he'd been taken to the hospital in time. The bullet had barely missed his heart.

"Mason, I want to thank you for what you did. You saved Sheila's life."

"Lianne, it was no problem. I happened to see him, and I just followed my instincts."

"The other thing is that we can't stay here any longer. I'm hoping there are no repercussions for

Taurean and the resort. We need to move somewhere safe. To another part of the island. We're
speaking to the local police right now."

"I have an idea. Taurean mentioned that he has
a beach house on the island. No one really knows
he's my brother, so it's unlikely they'll make a connection. You'll be able to go there. I'll ask him."

"I'm not sure he will agree, seeing that he may
not be too happy about what happened at his resort
today. However, the fewer people who know, the
better. I don't want to compromise. It's only about
a few days away from Clarkson's testimony.
Nothing can go wrong again."

"I'm going to make a call to return to active duty.
Hopefully, I'll be able to help in some way."

"I'll let my boss know, too. With one agent
down, another pair of hands would be perfect. You
can call your own boss and see what he says."

"Okay, give me all your relevant information.
I'll speak to him, but I'm sure he'll make all the
arrangements."

"You sure your leg is up to it?"

"No, I'm not sure, but my fingers work perfectly.
I'm not a marksman for nothing."

"Okay, if it's what you want to do. Give me the
info."

"Do you have paper?"

"Don't need it, just shoot. I have a good memory."

He rattled off the contact information she needed.

"Okay, take care of Sheila and Damien. I'll be back."

The man took the gun from the bag and stared at it. Damn, he was more than upset. He'd failed. The first time in his almost ten-year career that he'd failed. His disgust surged like bitter bile and he forced himself to kill the overwhelming feeling of loss and hopelessness.

He lifted the gun, caressing it like a willing woman. He'd let her down. He'd almost lost her, but in the chaos and confusion had been able to retrieve her. She needed the surge and the satisfaction of knowing that she was fulfilling her purpose.

Guns were like that. They had a spirit of their own and only someone like him who saw it as an extension of himself could appreciate the power and seduction of such a weapon.

There was an overpowering sexual gratification in holding the firm phallic symbol in his hand. Even now, he could still feel the steady throbbing.

He dropped the gun suddenly, not wanting to feel its power.

He needed a shower, needed to prepare for the second round. This time there would be no mistakes on his part.

He stripped his clothes, his arousal familiar. He turned the shower to cold.

This situation was more than he could handle. He definitely needed to take matters into his own hands.

Chapter 11

Hidden in the midst of dense mahogany trees, Taurean's beach house was the perfect hideaway. Mason was sure that any intruder would easily be spotted.

The only problem was having to remain indoors all day, a fact that Damien didn't like one bit. Mason had spoken to his boss and had been granted temporary assignment to work with Lianne and her team.

An unexpected sense of relief made him realize something about his life and all he'd done in the past fifteen years as an agent. He'd made a difference. Sam had made a difference. He may not have solved all his cases, but he'd helped to bring down some of the most notorious criminal minds. What he did was important.

He was needed.

He'd realized that the day he'd spotted a man about to take Sheila Clarkson out, and he'd played a part in saving her life, the life of another innocent person.

Most of all, the confines of the beach house put him in close proximity to Lianne. His intense awareness of her and the consuming attraction to her had forced him to face the truth.

He was in love with her.

He loved her.

In one short month—or was it less?—he was willing to give his heart and soul to a woman he barely knew. He wanted to spend his life with her, wanted to wake up to her smiling face each morning, wanted to hold their child in his hands.

There was so much about Lianne he loved. The way she walked, the way she dealt with a sad boy who missed his father. The way she'd sprinted after the man who'd tried to kill Sheila. Those were the things he'd grown to love about her.

Whenever Mason saw Taurean with Alana, he wished that same kind of happiness for himself. He'd even dared to think about marriage and images of a son and a daughter the spitting image of her mother.

Love was the strangest thing. For years he'd wondered if he'd ever find the right person. Yes, he'd had relationships, but he'd always wondered what it would be like to love someone with every fiber of his body.

Life was so unpredictable. One never knew what would happen. He'd always believed that he'd never fall in love with someone in the same profession. It was poetic justice that the first woman to make him think of forever and white picket fences happened to be in a highly dangerous job and he'd been the one to save her life.

He knew how dangerous his job was and hadn't believed he could handle a wife doing what he did. Strangely enough, he didn't feel this way around Lianne. For some reason, there was a certain confidence in her ability and the way she carried herself that made him realize she wouldn't do anything foolish. She oozed confidence and the way she'd reacted to the attack had made his admiration for her even greater. The reports he'd been sent on her had been the mere facts but underneath each comment he'd recognized the admiration of each of the writers.

There was the sound of footsteps behind him, and Mason slowly turned. She stood there. She looked different and he immediately realized it was how she was dressed. She wore a pair of jeans, a simple white shirt and the faint hint of a bulge told him she carried her gun. He'd been provided with one, too, and when he'd put it in his holster, he'd experienced that familiar sense of security. But the gun had become a part of who he was. He'd always dreaded the use of a gun, even after all these years; he didn't like them, but his job had emphasized the necessity of having one on. Unfortunately, the world he lived in was far from perfect.

"I just wanted to thank you for your quick actions the other day. If not, one of us may not have survived the attack. Despite my years in this job, that's the closest I've come to being killed. I don't know what would have happened if you weren't there."

"No thanks needed. I just did want I had to do. I've been trained to do it and it comes easy. My months away from work haven't slowed my reflexes. It's just this damn leg, but it's getting better."

"I realize that you *are* walking better."

"It only hurts when I make a sudden move, but beyond that it's fine. Are Damien and Sheila settled?"

"Yes, but they are going to remain in their room for a while. Sheila says they'll eat upstairs tonight, so I'll probably eat in my room, too. I'm feeling a bit tired."

"I'll retire early, too. I need to give my leg some rest."

"Well, I'll say good-night. I'll see you in the morning."

"Bye, sleep well," Mason replied. He watched as she disappeared around the corner.

Living in close proximity to Lianne could surely not be good for his libido.

He was tired, but there would be no sleep if his dreams about her continued tonight.

Definitely no sleep!

Carolyn walked slowly over to the bed and glanced down at her husband. She couldn't believe that she'd done it. Like a horny teenager, she'd jumped on a plane when Garth had suggested flying to Las Vegas. Eight hours later, a sapphire ring on her finger, she had been proclaimed Mrs. Garth Wade.

Now the wedding was over, she thought of the crazy thing she'd done and looked at the man she loved and knew that what she'd done was crazy, but it felt right, so very right. She remembered laughing with friends when Phyllis Windham had married a young man twenty years her junior, and had been saddened when, just two weeks later, she'd passed away.

She'd heard the insensitive rumor of Phyllis's inability to satisfy or keep up with her young and very virile husband. Carolyn didn't feel that way. Garth somehow made her feel younger, more alive.

In the past few weeks, she'd grown up. After John's death, she'd flirted and been utterly irresponsible when it came to men and relationships. Garth was willingly offering all she'd dreamed about. She knew that things wouldn't be easy but she shared Garth's determination to make this marriage work.

She wondered what Mason would be doing. Maybe she should call him and let him know. She scanned the hotel room, locating her cell phone nearby. She reached for it on the ground where it lay and quickly punched in the number. Mason answered on the second ring.

"Mason?"

"Yes, Mom? Who else do you expect to answer?"

"Sorry, force of habit. So how are things on the island? Still having a good time? Your leg? How is it holding up?"

"I'm enjoying the island. And the leg is getting stronger. I attended the doctor today. She's pleased with my progress."

"Good, Mason. However, I called because I have some news for you."

"News? Good news I hope?"

"Yes, it's good news."

There was a moment of silence.

"So are you going to tell me, Mom?"

"Yes." She hesitated and then said, "I got married last night."

"You got married!"

"Yes."

"To whom? Without telling me? Not to one of those young men from Europe?"

"No, Mason. He's a professor at the local university."

"A professor?"

"Yes, Mason, and he's a good man. Mason, I love him."

Her son hesitated. He didn't respond for a while.

"It's no problem, Mom. Once he treats you well and loves you. That's all I need to know."

"Yes, Mason, he's fine."

"Does he live in Bergen County, too?"

"Yes, in fact he lives on the other side of the lake."

"Mom, you mean he's rich? Why didn't you tell me?"

"Because I know my son would never consider money as a deciding factor of whether I get married or not."

"Sorry, Mom."

"Mason, you know me better than that. Despite all the bad things I've done, I've learnt my lesson. I love Garth."

"I should hope so, but why am I hearing about him after he became your husband? You must have known him for quite a while?"

"About three weeks. The same day I left you at the hospital. I met him in the park."

"Damn, Mom, are you crazy?"

"Now, Mason, don't be like that. He's a professor at the university. He's well-known. It's not like he's a mass murderer. I'm sure you'll get to know him when you return to the U.S."

"Okay, I can live with that." It really didn't make sense arguing since his mother was already married. He, however, had every intention of using his usual sources to find out about the man. "But I must meet him."

"Of course. Now that's settled. When are you planning to come home?"

"I'm not sure, Mom. I like it here. I told Taurean, my brother, who I am. He was a bit shocked at first, but we've been talking. He only had to look at my eyes to see who I was. I look a lot like him. His step-daughter, Melissa, is a sweetheart."

"Oh, that's great. I'm glad you didn't take my advice, but followed your heart. I'm sure your father would have wanted this to happen. What about your other brothers?"

"There are two other brothers. Daniel is a priest and lives in New York. Patrick and his wife live in Chicago. There was a younger brother. He died over ten years ago."

"I'm sorry to hear about that. But I'm still glad things turned out well."

"Yes, it did. I met a woman, too. She's nice. An

agent like I am. She's here on a case, but I can't say much about it right now."

"Oh, so this means there'll soon be grandchildren for me?"

"Mom, I've only just met her, but I really like her. I won't make any promises right now. I'm just seeing where it will go. So don't start buying gifts for the grandkids yet."

"Okay, I won't, but don't keep me waiting much longer, I'm not getting any younger."

When Carolyn felt the flicker of coolness at her ear, she knew it was time she told her son goodbye. Her husband was sure to want her undivided attention. With a promise to call again soon, she ended the conversation and turned to Garth.

The coolness had moved from her ear and made its way down to the crevice between her breasts.

"Mr. Wade, don't you know it's rude to interrupt your wife when she's chatting on the phone? Were you planning to embarrass me in front of my son?" she said in mock reprimand. "I'm going to have to spank you," she teased.

"Well, I'm all game for that. Didn't even know my wife was into all the kinky stuff."

"Well, I'm going to have to teach you a thing or two, lad."

Her husband didn't complain, but willingly participated as Carolyn gave him his first lesson for the day.

* * *

His mother had gone and got married!

Mason was going to do a bit of nosing around. He needed to find out about this Garth. His mother had been left a sizable fortune when his father… stepfather…had died, and he was sure that several of the men she'd had flings with had benefited financially from the relationship. He was sure she didn't know of the few occasions he'd lined the pockets of several of her suitors in order for them to disappear.

At first, his mother had disappointed him with her behavior the first few years after his stepfather's death. After a period of mourning, she'd transformed herself into a widow with not a care in the world.

And he'd been disgusted with her, until the night he'd found her crying and knew that all she showed the world was a well-constructed facade to hide her pain and loss.

That night, he'd held her in his arms as she'd cried for her husband and the years they'd had together. After that, she'd still had what she called "her attachments," but the endless nameless flirtations had come to an end.

But this marriage was a surprise. He knew the university, since it was his alma mater, but the man's name didn't ring a bell. Must be a new appointment? No fear, he had his ways of finding out what he wanted. Being an agent did have its advantages.

He heard a noise behind him and turned. It was Damien. Mason had almost expected Lianne. She had a strange habit of coming up behind him.

"Damien?" He noticed the boy's glum face. "What's the matter, son?"

"I'm bored. I want to go outside and play and Mom won't let me. I hate this. I hate my dad. It's his fault that we're here hiding."

Tears began to trickle down the boy's cheeks and Mason did not for the life of him know what to do. With the exception of Sam's two daughters and recently Melissa, he'd not had much contact with kids.

"Come here, sit next to me. Let me tell you a little secret about your dad. "

Damien sat next to him on the sofa.

"Do you know that your dad is one of the bravest men I know?"

"He is?"

"Yes, he is. Did your mom tell you why you're here on the island?"

"Yes, she told me that my dad has to testify."

"You know what that means?"

"Yes, that he has to go to court and tell the truth to get the bad man locked up."

"Good, and that makes your dad a brave, brave

man. If he doesn't tell the truth, the bad man may hurt someone else and I'm sure you won't want that to happen?"

"No, but I love my daddy and miss him. It's because he has to testify that's he not here."

"Yes, but he's soon going to be here. He wanted to do the right thing. I'm sure you know that doing the right thing is the best thing to do?"

"Yes, I'm sorry I said I hated him. Do you feel God will forgive me for saying so?"

"Yes, He knows you were angry and that you really don't hate your dad. And I think you're just like your dad. You're a brave little boy to be taking care of your mom."

Damien smiled. "And Lianne is a brave woman, because she's taking care of both of us. You know she's not my real nanny." He lowered his voice. "She's a cop who gets bad men. And she's making sure no bad men get us. Are you a cop, too?"

"Yes, we're both special cops."

"I want to be a cop when I grow up. I'm going to protect people from the bad men because I'm brave."

"Yes, you're sure brave. Want to go outside and kick some ball?"

"Yippee! I love soccer. My dad plays with me all the time." Suddenly his face fell. "Remember we can't go outside."

"No, it'll be all right. There are some other cops

watching us. You won't be able to see them, but they are making sure no one comes close to harm you."

"Oh, I'll go get my sneakers. I'm not supposed to play ball in slippers or with no shoes on."

"Okay, good, put them on and I'll tell your mom we're going outside for a while."

Before he could finish his words, Damien had raced upstairs.

Lianne sat with Sheila, watching as Damien and Mason kicked the ball back and forth. Mason, of course, favored his good leg, but she realized that his movements were stronger.

"So you like him?" Sheila said, her eyes probing.

Lianne's immediate thought was to deny it, but realized that it didn't make sense. "Yes, I think I'm falling for him…. Maybe it's a bit more than thinking."

"I know the feeling. I met Jason under the most unusual circumstance, but I was attracted to him from the beginning. By the end of the week I'd fallen in love."

"So the attraction was mutual?"

"No, definitely not! Jason didn't like me much. He thought I was arrogant and mean. But I knew I would marry him one day."

"And after that start, he eventually married you?"

"Yes, but not until a few years later when we met

again. By then I'd grown up. A lot of what he said about me was true. I was vain and self-centered. Fortunately, he didn't hold my past against me."

"He must be a wonderful man. Then and even now. To do what he's doing must take so much courage."

"At first he was so scared. He wanted to do it, but he was scared for us, Damien and me. I had to finally convince him that what he was doing was the right thing. I know my husband and know he would never have been happy if he'd just walked away. I couldn't do that to him. He would have felt less of a man if he'd walked away."

"You must miss him so much."

"I do, he's my best friend. He's the only man I've ever loved. I was fortunate he chose me. I could say he's fortunate, too. I think I've been the best wife I can be." Tears settled in her eyes and she struggled to compose herself. "Have you ever thought of getting married?"

"A few years ago, but it didn't work out. I found out, before it was too late, that he was sleeping with his secretary. I almost had one of those Lifetime movie moments. I came home early one day and almost witnessed him in bed with her. Thanks to a nosy neighbor, I was spared the embarrassment. I just walked away and never looked back."

"I can see why you're not too enthused about marriage. It can't be easy finding out the person you love is cheating. I'm not sure I could have walked out. I'd probably have castrated him immediately. You can only hope things last."

"Mason is the first person since then that I've looked beyond the first date. He has a reputation of being a good agent. One of the best in fact. He seems an honorable man."

"He's noble just like you. Though Mason seems quiet and reserved, he can be lots of fun. I'll never forget last night."

"I know what you mean. I still have images of him rolling on the floor in laughter."

"You're perfect for each other. The two of you have so much in common."

"I'm not sure about that. When we talked about his career, he wasn't too happy. I know his partner died a few months ago. That's how his leg was hurt."

"Since he's here means that he must have changed his mind. He's like you. Neither of you will be able to stop doing good. Going after the criminals and protecting the world from evil will always motivate you and Mason. What each of you does can only be considered noble."

Lianne thought about what Sheila was saying. To be honest, a lot of it was true. There was something noble in what they did. When she was growing up, she'd wanted to be a cop, but special intelligence had drawn her in when she'd watched a movie on television featuring agents. She didn't regret her choices in life. Her only regret was not having children, but her job was so dangerous, she didn't want to leave any children on their own without even a father to take care of them. In a dangerous job like hers, you never thought about dying, but it was very much a reality.

"Sheila, what you say is so true. I've never really thought about it in terms of nobility, but I know that I've always wanted to help others. Save them from the evils of the world."

There was laughter in the distance and they turned to watch Damien and Mason as they rolled upon the ground.

He was good with kids, despite telling her he wasn't. She'd seen him with Damien in the past few days and she'd seen the way he was with Melissa. He'd fallen into the role of uncle with the kind of energy and commitment he did for everything else. She stared at him, noticing the strength in his body.

His left leg still appeared a bit awkward, but it had regained its muscular tone and almost looked the perfect pair again. She liked how he looked in the shorts that he'd traded with the long track bottoms she'd grown so accustomed to seeing him in when he walked on the beach or went swimming. She liked how his upper body showed evidence of his fitness level, with his broad shoulders and well-defined arms.

What embarrassed her most was her inability to keep her eyes off his well-defined six-pack and the hint of curly hair that disappeared into his shorts. Her eyes never failed to notice the slight bulge of his manhood.

"So, do you plan to eat him sometime soon?" Sheila teased. "You'd actually forgotten that I'm here."

Lianne joined in the laughter, refusing to be embarrassed by her train of thought or the fact that she'd been caught in the act of lusting.

"No need to be embarrassed. I was doing a bit of lusting myself. I'm going to have to confess when I see my husband in a few days."

"You must have some regrets about all this."

"Of course, I do, but they really don't matter. When Jason and I made the decision, we put all the regrets behind. I don't know what the plan is but I'm sure we'll find out soon. We go into witness protection, so it'll be a serious period of adjustment. At least we'll be together. That's all that matters."

"You must miss him."

"Yes, I do, but I try not to show it. I have to be strong for Damien."

"I hope I find what you have one day."

"I'm sure you will. It may be sooner than you think."

Another round of laughter came from the two playing on the beach.

"Who wants to go in the water? I've been aching to take a swim."

Nodding her head, Lianne stood, kicked her slippers off, dropped the shirt she wore over her swimsuit and followed Sheila, who was already racing across the sand.

On reaching the water's edge, Sheila leaped into the air and dived gracefully into the water. Lianne followed suit, diving in equally as gracefully, and swimming swiftly to where Sheila now floated on her back. She tilted her head in the direction of the beach to see Mason slipping from his shorts, revealing a close-fitting swim trunk. Slightly ahead, Damien plunged into the water, his dive lacking the grace the women had demonstrated, but his laughter was infectious. It was the first time since his arrival on the island that she'd heard him laugh with such abandonment. Yes, he'd laughed before, but this time she knew it came right from the core of his body.

"Come, Mason," he screamed. "I want to see you dive, too."

Lifting his injured leg slightly off the ground, Mason tilted expertly over and flipped into the water.

"Boy, that was great. Can you teach me how to do that?" Damien asked.

"Of course, but when you're a bit older and can swim better. A move like that could easily hurt you, so I don't want you to try it yet."

"Okay, Mason, but it was way cool. Can you do it again?"

Mason obliged; this time he jumped into the air and flipped twice before he entered the water.

"Wow, awesome. You're way cool, Mason. Wait till I learn how to do that. My friends will be envious."

Sheila glanced over to where they were and Lianne followed. She watched as Sheila joined them and soon they were playing an aquatic version of tag. Sheila was trying to catch Damien when Lianne realized that the body moving swiftly in the water beside her was Mason. She swam quickly, but despite his leg, he easily gained on her, grabbed her leg and pulled her toward him. Holding her head gently, he forced it underwater briefly before he allowed her to rise.

"I win," Mason said.

"Yes, you did. I'm not much of a swimmer, but you're good."

"Yes, I wasn't on the varsity team for nothing. Went to college on a swimming scholarship. Almost made the Olympic team one year, but got hurt. By the next Olympics I was already in the agency and undercover."

"I'm surprised. Your leg has been improving quickly. All of the long walks and swimming seems to have helped."

"Yes, the island couldn't have been a better place for healing. My recovery is much faster than my doctor anticipated, but I had no intentions of being out of commission for too long. I hate to be weak."

As he spoke, Lianne suddenly became aware of his closeness. Pressed again him, she could feel his arousal under the water. Her cheeks reddened.

Her eyes met his and she saw the same awareness that she knew was visible in her own eyes.

"See what you do to me, Miss Thomas?"

"Me," she replied coyly. "I have no idea what you're talking about."

"Maybe I'll have to show you another time."

"Maybe you will."

When Mason glided away, Lianne's space suddenly felt empty. Nearby, voices cleared. She looked around, noticing Sheila's smug expression.

What had she gotten herself into?

Chapter 12

During the night, Lianne could not sleep. Not because of the Clarkson situation. She was troubled by her powerful response to Mason. She wondered what he was doing right now. She'd decided to go to bed early, tired by the activities of the day. Damien had fallen asleep while watching television and Sheila had taken him up, informing Lianne that she too would be retiring for the night. Mason had gone up to his room after their swim and had not reappeared.

She knew it was because of his leg. When leaving the beach, Lianne had noticed that he'd been limping slightly. He'd overdone it and was now suffering the consequences.

Lianne rose from the bed, the cool night air causing her to shiver. Despite the island's heat during the day, the breeze off the ocean at nights often had a slight chill. She walked over to the window, her eyes flickering around, but there was nothing out of the ordinary. Somewhere out there, hidden in the shadows, two agents kept watch, so the likelihood of any harm coming to them was at a minimum.

For now, they were safe.

She hoped.

Lianne yawned. She was tired, but her eyes refused to comply with her weary mind. Maybe a cup of warm milk would help.

Slipping on her slippers next to the bed, Lianne exited the room and moved quietly down the stairs, hoping the occasional creak wouldn't wake anyone.

When she reached the kitchen, she flipped the switch on and headed to the refrigerator. There was a familiarity in this routine. Since joining the agency, she'd had many sleepless nights that only hot milk could help. Anytime a case was particularly danger-ous or hinted at uncertainty, she couldn't sleep.

And falling in love with Mason Sinclair didn't help the situation.

Behind her, the floor creaked.

With years of experience on her side, she turned swiftly, her body tense for the attack.

Mason.

"Damn, don't you know better than to come up on someone like that? Hell, you're an experienced agent."

"Sorry, couldn't sleep. I didn't know that someone was down here until I saw the light on. I thought someone had left the lights off when everyone retired."

"Sorry, Mason, I overreacted. I'm a bit jittery from the other day. Want some warm milk?"

"I'd prefer a cup of tea, but I'll take care of it."

"Tea?"

"Yes, tea. My father's influence. He passed on the love of a good English tea to me. Barbados has been quite accommodating in that respect. I get all the tea I want here."

Lianne filled the kettle and plugged it in, then searched for a cup and glass. She opened the refrigerator, took the milk carton out and filled her mug. She sat on one of the stools at the counter.

Lianne watched Mason as he quickly made his cup of tea. He came over, sitting on the stool next to where she sat.

"So you can't sleep either?"

"No, I rarely get any sleep when I'm on a case."

"I know what you mean."

"And though everything seems all right, I'm sure the man is going to try again. Cordoni won't give up."

"I feel the same way. I know he's going to try again, but we have to be better prepared this time."

"We will be. If not for you, I'd have a dead client on my hands. I wouldn't have been able to live with that."

"Lianne, don't beat yourself up this way. You did a fine job. By the way, how's the agent that was shot?"

"Smart? He'll live. Only a collapsed lung, but he's doing fine now."

"Glad to hear. I was really worried about him."

"I was, too. I've grown fond of him and Monroe. When you have a partner, it's not easy working with others. I've enjoyed working with them and I'm sure Brian feels the same way," Lianne said.

"It's becoming more difficult each year to find good agents. I've been rethinking leaving the Bureau. Who's going to do this work if we don't, if we all decide to leave?"

Lianne didn't respond. There was no need to. She knew exactly what Mason meant. Her motivation would always be the desire to see justice for those innocent persons who became prey to sick predators.

For a while the only sound was the beating of their hearts and the occasional clicking of a spoon against a teacup.

Mason put his cup down and said, "I think I'm

going to go up now. It's been a long day and I need to get some sleep."

"Okay, let me wash the cups and then I'll follow you up."

She quickly washed what they had used and followed him as he moved out of the room, along the corridor and up the stairs.

When they reached his room, he turned to her and said, "I've not been completely honest with you. Yes, the case is bothering me a bit, but one of the reasons I can't sleep has to do with a lovely black woman I can't get off my mind."

"And who may that be?" she asked.

"Do you need to ask?"

Without warning, he placed his arms around her waist and drew her to him. For the briefest of moments, an awareness of the inevitable sparked between them, and then his lips found hers.

His lips touched her in a tentative probe, as if he wanted to sample what she was so willingly giving but realized that the moment was special. He intensified the kiss, tasting and teasing her with his tongue, causing her to shiver against him.

Her hands found their way under his shirt, wanting to feel the hardness of his body.

She felt him tremble when her left hand touched a rigid nipple, kneading it between her fingers until he groaned.

"You sure you want to do this out here? I'm sure your room will be better."

"You sure about this, Lianne? I want you so much, but you have to feel it's right, know it's right."

"Yes, I'm sure. If you don't take me inside soon, I won't be responsible for what I'll do. And I'm sure you don't want Sheila or Damien to come outside and see us here."

"No, we can't have that, can we?"

He opened the door of his room, allowing her to enter, then quickly followed her and closed the door behind himself.

His bed beckoned.

He held her hand, taking her with him to the bed.

"Let me slip these off you."

She raised her hands, allowing him to take her T-shirt off. Expecting him to take her jeans off next, she almost screamed when his mouth closed on one dusky nipple.

"Mason, what are you trying to do to me?"

When he lifted his head to respond, she silenced him by guiding his head back to the already aching nipple.

She felt his warm hand against her hip, drawing her closer to him, and it was only then that she realized her skirt was off.

"Get on the bed. I'll undress."

She obeyed, watching as he slipped from his track shorts. Her eyes flew immediately to his erection. He was big, but there was something strong and noble about the way his manhood stood erect for her.

She beckoned to him, gripping his behind firmly when he stood before her. She closed her mouth on him, tasting the salty tang of his essence. Mason groaned.

"Don't. You'll have me done in a second. I don't want our first time to be over so quickly. I haven't done this in a while so my control is off-kilter."

He lowered himself onto her, loving the feel of her arms around him.

When she wrapped her legs around him, he was amazed by how perfect she felt. Her body writhed with pleasure and he knew he could wait no longer. Leaving her briefly, he searched in the drawer of the bedside chest and found the foil package.

He handed her the condom, standing as she rolled it onto his hardness. He groaned.

When she was done, he watched her for a while as she lay on her back before him, her legs slightly parted as if eager to welcome him.

When he lowered onto her, he slipped smoothly inside her, almost coming undone by her warm tightness.

She immediately wrapped her legs around him, allowing him deeper penetration, and when she started the dance of centuries of lovers, he knew that he'd found the place he'd been searching for. With every thrust, he felt her grip him, her womanhood responding fervently to his movement. Lianne moved with him, a husky groan of pleasure joining his more vocal expression.

He was a vocal lover, wanting to tell her how she made him feel, wanting to tell her he loved her.

With each stroke, he could feel the pressure building, the moment of release closer than he wanted. He felt her tighten, her body shaking with the convulsions, and the intensity of her own orgasm took him over the edge, until they both screamed with the force of what had just happened between them.

In the aftermath of their lovemaking, their breathing ragged, he thought he heard her say, "I love you."

When he turned to her, her eyes were closed. She appeared asleep and he realized it was only his imagination.

Her eyes closed, Lianne felt like kicking herself. How could she have blurted out what she had?

She felt his arms around her and Mason drew nearer. She could learn to love this. Maybe it was time she took a chance on love.

Maybe Mason was the right one?

Maybe.

* * *

Lianne groaned when the water spouted from the nozzle, stinging her with its coldness. God, it felt so good. She'd awoken fifteen minutes ago to find Mason gone. She'd expected it since they didn't want anyone to find out about what was going on. Until the assignment was over, they would have to be content with their nights together. She smiled. Here she was planning ahead and she wasn't even sure if there would be a repeat of last night.

Last night.

All she could say was *incredible*. She'd fallen asleep after the first round of lovemaking only to wake up an hour later to Mason's mouth on her breast and a raging arousal pressed against her. She immediately guided him into her, pleasured by the feel of the length and thickness of his manhood. Having him inside her made her feel as if she'd found the other half of her whole.

But then, she'd taken control, moving on top of him and taking him on a ride he'd never forget. It had not ended there. Twice more during the night, they'd awoken to their mutual need and like horny teenagers had given into the raging passion burning between them.

Now, with the water soothing her sore muscles, she ached not only from the overactivity but because she wanted him again.

She really wasn't too sure what was happening to her, but she knew beyond a shadow of a doubt that she loved Mason Sinclair. It was not the love they made that convinced her, but the way they'd made love. She'd been half in love with him already, but the passion and intensity of their love-making had made her realize their compatibility existed on more than one level.

Lianne knew her heart's fragility, and making the move from friend to lover had been a hard one. She had not hesitated in accepting the invitation to his room. In fact, she'd been the one to make the first move. She'd wondered during the past days what she would do if the opportunity ever arose for them to make love.

She'd known that she would not refuse. Even if they left the island of Barbados and lost contact, she'd at least have had the memories. Now, she was sure she'd never be able to get Mason from her mind or her soul. With his eyes, hands, lips and…that, too, he'd made her his, body and soul.

Lianne turned the shower off and stepped out of the cubicle. Instinctively, she moved toward the window. In the distance, down by the beach, Damien and Mason were knee deep in the sand. Before them was one of the largest sand castles she'd ever seen. She took her watch up, glancing at the time—1:00 p.m. She hadn't realized it was so late. On duty and she'd overslept.

She scrambled quickly into her T-shirt and blue jeans and slipped from the room.

Downstairs she moved to the kitchen; the spicy flavor of something cooking drew her. Sheila was there, engrossed in what she was doing.

"Whatever you're doing smells great."

Sheila turned, her eyes moving immediately to Lianne's face, a sly smile on her face.

"I'm making spaghetti and meatballs with a special family recipe for the meatballs. I hope you're hungry." She laughed. "At least, I'm sure you're hungry."

Lianne knew her face was as red as it could get.

"No need to deny it. My advice. If you don't want anyone to know of your nightly activities, don't scream too loudly. But don't worry, Damien didn't lose a wink."

"I'm so embarrassed. Did I really make that much noise?"

"Just pulling your leg. I went to the bathroom during the night and heard some strange noises, but knew exactly what was going on. I won't even ask, since your cries of ecstasy have already told me that you totally enjoyed it."

Deciding there was no need to play coy, Lianne said, "Sheila, it was amazing. I didn't realize that making love could be so intense. I'm not a virgin, but making love to Mason was more than I imagined."

"That's how you know you've found the right person. Before Jason, there were a few others, but none ever rocked my world as he did. He doesn't even have to touch me and I'm ready to go crazy."

"I know what you mean. I'm beginning to have the same experience."

"Yes, it's called being in love," Sheila said.

Lianne did not reply. What Sheila had said was absolutely true. She was utterly and completely in love with Mason Sinclair.

"Love comes at the most unexpected time, doesn't it? Lianne, maybe it's time you listen to your heart."

"I think I'm learning to. I've decided to see where this goes. I owe myself a chance at happiness. I'm not going to throw it away," Lianne commented.

"Good, then that's settled. You can go call the boys. Lunch is almost done. At least if you can tear them away from the mansion they're making."

Leaving Sheila adding the final touches to a tasty-looking Caesar salad, Lianne headed out the door and down to the beach.

When she reached Mason and Damien, they looked up. She tried hard not to look directly at

Mason, but she couldn't help it. Their eyes clashed, flames ignited and she felt that now-familiar heat warm her body.

"Lunch is ready. Sheila says you must come now."

"Yippee! I'm so hungry. Come, Mason, let's go. Mom's the best-est cook. Better even than my granny."

"Okay, bud, you run on. I have to move a bit slower than you do."

Damien raced off as if he were in the finals of the Olympic one-hundred meter.

Lianne turned to walk away.

"So you're not going to walk with me and keep me company?" Mason asked.

Lianne stopped, waiting for him to catch up. Her heart raced. "If you want me to."

"Of course, I want you to. I hope you're not embarrassed about what happened last night."

"I'm a big girl. I can handle it. Are you?"

"Am I what? Embarrassed? No. A bit tired? Definitely, but that's expected," he responded. He moved closer, his face showing his concern. "Are you okay?"

"Okay? What do you mean?" she replied, then blushed when she realized what he meant. "I'm fine," she reassured him.

"I'm glad. I was a bit worried." He reached out and touched her cheek. "Lianne, before we go back to the house, I need to say something. I don't want what happened to us to be just a holiday memory, a one-night fling. When this situation is all over we'll talk. I need more than one night."

"I need more than one night, too," she replied. "And yes, we'll talk when this is all over."

"Want to come to my room again tonight?" he asked, his voice holding the promise of another night of passion.

"Yes, but only if you promise not to make too much noise. I'm sure you won't want to keep Sheila awake another night."

It was Mason's turn to look embarrassed.

"She heard us?" he groaned.

"Yeah, she did. Every moan and groan. But make sure you're not so noisy next time," she teased.

"So I'm the one who made the noise last night. Your memory of last night's activities definitely varies from mine. Tonight, I'll be sure to show you the truth."

"I look forward to it, Mr. Sinclair."

Night came like a thief, creeping up on Lianne unexpectedly. After lunch, she'd decided to take a short nap. Monroe had left his position on the outskirts of the property and given her an update on the situation. Clarkson was scheduled to testify the next day since the other prosecution witnesses had all testified.

Now, Lianne sat on the sand. She was looking

forward to getting back her life. She would miss Sheila and Damien, but their situation demanded the reality of witness protection.

Above, dark clouds covered the sky, allowing the merest hint of the moon above. Despite the threat of a rainstorm, Lianne gave in to the overwhelming need to come outdoors.

In the distance, a cruise ship made its way south, its bright lights twinkling like the few stars in the sky. And then the clouds parted.

The moonlight, glad to finally work its magic, cast its ray upon everything in sight.

In the distance a dog barked. Beach came immediately to mind, but she knew it couldn't be Mason's homeless friend.

To her left, the sand crunched, and she quickly glanced in the direction of the noise.

Mason.

Somehow, she knew he'd come. She almost willed him to her, wanting to spend time with him.

In the moonlight, shadows played with his usually strong features, making them gentler, softer.

"Lovely night, isn't it?" he observed. "This is my favorite time of the day."

"I've noticed. It's the time you run. The time you sit on the rocks thinking."

"Yes, and dreaming," he said.

"So you're a dreamer, too."

"Don't we all have our dream?" he asked.

"Maybe, but I've stopped dreaming. Reality comes too often to bite us on the ass when dreams that may be too fanciful try to distract you from the truth about life."

"Truth about life? What's the truth about life?" he questioned.

"That the world is a cruel place. Look at Clarkson. He had a perfect life. A wife and son who loves him. The perfect job, the proverbial picket fence and look where that's put him. Almost dead. His wife, his son, his life will never ever be the same again. In two days, he'll have lost all he had." She felt angry at the wrong done to the Clarksons.

"But he has what's important to him. His wife and child. That's what will make all that he's done worthwhile."

She laughed. "Isn't it ironic? You came here full of anger and disillusioned about your work and now you talk of dreams. I have no time for dreaming."

"Maybe that's why you're so cynical about life. You have no dreams. That's why you're lonely each night in bed. You don't dare to dream for happiness." She could hear the anger in his voice.

She stood to leave, unwilling to hear the truth of what he said. He reached out, holding her, refusing to let her leave.

"You think I don't know that you only give me a part of yourself, that each time we made love last night that you held back a part of yourself?"

She didn't respond.

"You want to know what I want most in life. It's to find a woman I love more than life itself. I've never seen that in any aspect of my life. Yes, I knew my mother loved my father. Not my real father, Joshua Buchanan, but the man that raised me as his son. They loved each other. There were times, I believed that my mother dishonored what she had with him when she started getting involved with her boy toys, but I realized something. That she was human, that for a moment, those men helped her to forget that he wasn't here anymore. Was it bad? Maybe, but do I understand why she did what she did? Absolutely."

She seemed surprised by his declaration, and pulled away from him, knowing that his touch would only make her think of the dreams he'd placed in her mind. "But I'm not sure if that's what I want for myself. I'd have to give up part of who I am. Isn't that what a relationship is about?"

"Do you want to get married? Have kids?"

She did not respond immediately.

"Answer me, Lianne. Tell me how you feel," Mason pleaded.

"For a long time, I didn't have that as a plan for

my life. I'd seen my mother and father's life together and felt it wasn't for me. Maybe that has changed a bit now. But I'm still not sure I want to commit myself wholly and solely to a man. I feel as if I'll lose a part of who I am. I'll lose myself to you." Lianne wanted him to understand, but she knew her words were not what he wanted hear.

"Maybe you're beginning to dream, wish for more than what you thought was enough. When I was young, my dad and I used to lie in the backyard and watch the stars, but I always found the moon the most fascinating."

"Why?"

"I see the moon as a place where our dreams lie and all we have to do is call on those dreams and maybe they'll come true. My father always said, 'Son, just as you enjoy the sun and rain, embrace the moonlight.' I only now understand the significance of what he meant."

Lianne looked up, the moon's brilliance startling. And then it was gone, the clouds covering it again.

She shivered.

What Mason said was true. She knew she was being stubborn.

"I want more from you, Lianne. I don't just want an island romp between the sheets."

Lianne's heart stopped. She could already hear his words; knew that what he would say would be a reflection of her own vulnerability, but she couldn't say the words.

"Damn, woman, do you realize I love you?"

She'd expected *want* and *need* but never *love*.

She breathed in deeply and counted to five, but still she could not put her own thoughts into words.

"Sorry, I didn't mean to blurt that out, but that's how I feel. In the midst of all the confusion that's my life, I know I love you."

She turned from him, again unsure of what to say. When she looked back, she saw the hurt in his eyes.

"I'm not sure what to say. I enjoy being with you, like you. Making love with you is more than I could imagine. But I don't want to talk about love."

"You don't have to. Just marry me and I'll show you how good it can be, that what we have is right."

"Mason, don't do this to me," she pleaded. "You know I'm not ready for marriage. I'm not even sure if I'm ready for love. What we have is good, let's enjoy it while it lasts."

"So does this mean that all this is over in the next two days when you return to your life and I to mine?"

"I'm not saying that. We live close enough that we can stay in contact. I'm just not ready for marriage right now. I have so many plans in relation to my career."

"Oh, you do have your dreams. They just don't

involve love." She could hear the disappointment in his voice, the anger boiling beneath the surface. "I think I'm going to bed. I won't be good company for the rest of the night."

He looked upward and then pointed at the sky. "See, the moon's hidden." With that he walked away.

Lianne wanted to run after him, she wanted to shout, "I love you," but to do that would ruin all her dreams for her future. Mason was right; she did have dreams, but just not the same dreams he had.

For years, her career had been all she'd wanted. She'd lived for the agency, and for her that had been enough. Relationships were complicated. Her parents had been married for fifteen years before she'd been born and when she'd turned ten, they'd divorced. Twenty-five years of marriage and love died. What hope was there for love and marriage in this age of technology and fast living?

For years, she'd been pulled from her mother to her father. Her mother had moved to England and the summers had all been spent there, but she'd missed the stability that came with a home with both parents.

What hope did she and Mason have? Ironically, they were in the same field of work, but there the compatibility ended.

Or did it?

She didn't know much about what he liked and what he didn't. She just knew he was an honest, brave man. Maybe when she returned to the U.S. she could let them explore the possibilities.

But she was so afraid to love.

Her mind kept telling her that it wasn't love just the good companionship and the incredible sex. That had her feeling this way.

But her heart was beating a different tune.

She was in love.

Mason slammed the door behind himself and listened as it echoed inside his head. He'd never been as frustrated as he was tonight. Lianne had made him absolutely angry.

How could she be content with what little they had? How could she not want more than the love-making? Didn't she want forever?

He'd seen so many examples of love in action during his lifetime. His mother and his father, John, Sam and Clair and now Taurean and Alana. He wanted love like that for himself. He did not want to die old and lonely.

Maybe his dreams were a bit out of his reach. Like the moon…too far to embrace.

But he would fight for her. She had feelings for him, that much he knew. He was sure that the intensity of her response to his lovemaking was evidence of her attraction to him.

So what was the problem?

It was this feminist thing that seemed to obsess women of the twentieth and twenty-first centuries.

But no, he wouldn't go there. He appreciated women who were strong and confident. A soft, dependent woman would never do for him. Even his mother was that independent, in charge type of woman. His mother had never, ever been a wimp. She'd never been controlling, but she'd always had her own opinion on things and Mason had enjoyed many a debate between his parents on world affairs, religion, music, anything of interest. As a young teenager he'd been encouraged to join in the discussions.

He definitely didn't want a wimp.

He walked over to the window, but could not see Lianne from his room.

He had to do something to change her mind before he left Barbados. There was no way that he'd give up on what he felt for this amazing woman.

Tonight, he'd be alone, but she too would be thinking about what could have been. And in the middle of the night when he was aching, he knew that she'd be aching just the way he was.

That much he knew.

For the next few days, he'd do everything in his power to show Lianne Thomas that she couldn't live without him.

In the distance, he could see the moon, its glow

touching all around it. He reached his hand out, feeling its energy. Maybe he was being a bit corny, but somehow he felt the need to reach out and grasp his dream, embrace the moonlight.

He stood there for what seemed like hours, and when he finally moved from the window and slipped between the sheets, the ache was still there, but he felt the power of his dream and he knew that everything would be all right.

Time had a way of taking care of things.

When he eventually fell asleep, a smile on his face, the scent of the woman he loved still lingered in the room.

Chapter 13

Lianne slowly came awake, an uneasy feeling causing her to reach immediately for her weapon. The night was still, too still. The familiar noises could not be heard.

Something was definitely wrong.

Someone was out there.

She slipped her hand under the bed, feeling the cold steel of the gun in her hand.

Rising from the bed, she pulled her nearby track pants on and moved quickly to the bedroom door. She pushed the door slowly open. No noise.

She stopped, listening for any unusual sounds in the silence.

Then she heard it. A single creak in the midst of the silence.

An intruder?

"Lianne?" Her name was a whisper, but she could tell it was Mason.

"Mason, I heard a noise downstairs and was about to come check it out. You heard it, too."

"Yes," his said, his voice was low, controlled.

"I'll check the front of the house, you check the back. Be careful."

"I will, you, too. We'll meet back in the kitchen."

In the darkness, they slipped downstairs, unable to see each other clearly. At the bottom of the stairs, the light of the full moon above illuminated the room, making it easier to see each other. Lianne turned left, glancing back as Mason moved toward the back of the house.

Lianne placed her back against the wall, moving slowly toward the sitting room. When she reached the entrance, she heard the noise again; this time she realized it came from the direction of the kitchen. Slipping inside the room, she placed her back against the wall just at the entrance, hoping the intruder would pass by.

Outside the room, the shadow paused and then the footsteps moved away, heading in the direction of the stairs.

Lianne slipped quietly from the room. The man stood at the bottom of the stairs. She could not see him clearly, but a flash of light in his hand made her aware of the weapon he carried.

Lianne moved quickly, willing him not to look back. He didn't as he remained focused on reaching the stairs.

A noise from the direction Mason had taken caused him to turn abruptly, giving her the chance she needed. She inhaled deeply and then jumped into action, springing the short distance to where he stood. She kicked out, but he moved smoothly, the blow barely grazing his cheek. He spun around and pointed his gun at her, but her other leg was already in the air, knocking the gun flying. He dived to the ground, reached for it, but realizing she carried a gun, he rolled along the floor trying to blend into the darkness.

Then she heard a loud thud and saw him lying unconscious flat on the ground and Mason standing over him with his cane in his hand, a broad smile on his face.

"Didn't even have to use the gun, I just whacked him with my cane. Was too simple."

Lianne laughed in response. "How can you joke at a time like this?"

"Lianne, my dear, all part of the program. Since I did all the hard work, you can find some rope and tie him up until the police get here. I'll call them. I'll call Monroe on his cell phone. I'm not sure how he was able to get by him again, but he did."

"I'll go wake Sheila and let her know what happened."

"Good. We work well together, don't we?"

"Yes, we do. You go take care of the cops. I'll get this sorted out."

As the sun reared its head from behind the horizon, Lianne watched as the local police carried away the man who'd been hired by Cordoni to get rid of Sheila and Damien. He'd not succeeded, but the effect on Sheila had been hard.

But now it was almost over.

Jason Clarkson was scheduled to give his testimony early in the morning and soon it would be over. By tomorrow, Sheila and Damien would be on their way to meet him and start their new life. Lianne was not totally sure of what life they would have, but she hoped all would turn out for the best. Maybe in prison, Cordoni's influence would wane.

Today was a day of endings. In a day or two she'd be back home and back at her desk doing what she did best. Mason would remain on the island to spend some time with his new family.

If not for him, they may not have captured the hit man, and for that she was grateful.

There was a noise behind her and she turned to see Mason.

"Sheila and Damien will be leaving soon. They are just getting their stuff together and they'll be taken elsewhere. Your job is over. Other agents have taken over. I'm not even sure if they'll be taken back to the U.S. first." The information came to her like a monologue of factual information. She could tell he was trying to keep his distance.

"I'll be leaving soon to go back to the resort. Taurean is picking me up. You can ride back with us or one of the police vehicles will take you."

"No, I'll go back with you if Taurean doesn't mind."

"I've already told him, so it's fine. Maybe we can talk later tonight."

"I'd like that," she replied. "Are you sure?"

"Yes, I'm sure. *We will talk*. In the meantime, Sheila and Damien want to see you. You need to go before they leave."

"Sure, I'll go now."

She left the room, looking back at him before he disappeared.

When she reached Sheila's room, she knocked and the door immediately flung open.

"Come in, Lianne, I'm just finishing up my packing. I just received a call from Jason. He has testified and everything seems in place for us to move on to our next home." Her voice was soft, troubled.

Lianne moved toward her. She placed her hand on Sheila's shoulder. "Sheila, everything is going to be all right."

"I know. We're not the first people to go into witness protection, but it's going to be hard to leave my family and friends. Jason and I discussed this when he finally decided to testify, and it seemed so easy. Now that the time is here, it's not as easy as I thought." Her voice cracked. Lianne could see the early flush of tears.

"Sheila, you're one of the bravest women I know and I know Jason possesses that same strength of character. I know both of you will be fine."

By now the tears were coming quickly and Lianne moved to sit beside her on the bed. She placed her arms around this woman who'd somehow become her friend. Sadness inside threatened to overwhelm her, but she knew that this was the best thing for them to do. Ironically, she had her first real friend and now she was back on her own.

For a while they sat there; no words were necessary. Only two women who'd grown to care for each other and understood the special bond that existed between two friends.

There was a knock on the door and Damien entered, followed by Monroe.

"It's time to go, Mrs. Clarkson. The vehicle is here."

Sheila stood, her body shaking. She turned to Lianne, placing her hands around her and holding her tight.

"I'm going to miss you."

"Me, too. I know things are going to be different, but you have a husband that loves you and a great son."

"I know," she said. And then she whispered in Lianne's ear. "You're going to find love, too. Just trust your heart."

"I will," Lianne responded. She wished she could stop her own tears.

A few minutes later, she stood at the window watching the white police car as it made its way down the driveway before disappearing around a corner.

She wished the Clarksons the best.

Now, she had to take care of her own problem.

Mason Sinclair.

When Mason knocked at the door and entered the bedroom, Lianne stood at the window. He knew she'd be watching the car as it drove away.

She did not move, so he made his way to her and immediately placed his arms around her.

Their time together would soon be over. He'd sent the other agents along, asking them to leave a car behind so that he and Lianne could make their way back to the resort.

"We have the house all to ourselves. Want to play hooky? Let's go to the beach and then we can spend the rest of the day making hot sweaty love."

There was nothing she would like to do more, but she hesitated, wondering if she would be making a mistake.

To hell with it.

She wanted the man.

"Why don't we just spend the day in bed and make love. I've been to the beach more times in the past few weeks, so I can surely miss a day, unless you really want to go."

"Oh, we could skip the beach, but I'd like to get some breakfast first and then I'm all yours."

A few hours later, Mason sat on the deck chair next to where Lianne lay asleep. Relaxed, she appeared less intense, but beautiful nevertheless. Strange, he'd never expected that in four short weeks, his life would have changed so much. When he'd arrived on the island, he'd been unsure about the rest of his life. Now, he knew what he wanted most.

A life with Lianne.

Wanted to wake up in the morning next to her; wanted to have wonderful children with her. Most important, he wanted to spend the rest of his life with her as a lover and friend. He knew there was so much about her he still didn't know. About her family, her childhood, what had inspired her to join the Bureau?

He watched as she moved, her firm breasts inviting him to sample. As he watched her, he felt that now-familiar jolt of fire course through his body and he struggled to control his growing arousal.

Lianne's eyes flickered open and immediately saw him. Pools of liquid brown sparked with desire and he knew she wanted him as much as he wanted her.

"Lianne," he said, "I need to have you now."

He rose from his seat, lifted her in his arms and walked slowly to the house. As he walked, he felt the gentlest of kisses on his neck and the coldness of her tongue tickling his ears, and it took all his willpower not to lay her on the ground and make love to her there.

In the bedroom, he watched as she undressed, tossing her clothes to the floor before she sat on the bed waiting for him to join her. Slipping out of his own clothes, he could feel her eyes on him. He felt vulnerable and exposed as he took his shorts off and his manhood sprang to life.

Lianne reached for him, drawing him to her, until he could feel her breasts against his chest.

Without warning, she flipped him onto his back, pinning him to the bed.

And then she made love to him. That slow, toe-curling kind of lovemaking only a woman who knew her man could achieve. She didn't leave an inch of his body untouched, delighted when she found his most sensitive spots.

When she reached for the last condom that rested on the chair next to the bed, he smiled, content to let her take control.

Her exploration of his body had left him tired, so he had no complaints.

Before she sheathed him, she took him in her mouth, teasing and driving him crazy until he almost reached the point of no return...and she stopped.

"Sorry, Mason Sinclair, but I want you to make love to me."

Mason watched as she lowered herself onto him, feeling his muscles clench and unclench as he entered her slowly. His manhood throbbed, responding to the silky feel of her womanhood.

And then she started a slow, tantalizing rotation of her lower body, causing his hips to jerk upward, joining her and matching each stroke with a thrust of his own.

Upward, downward, upward, downward.

Lianne groaned with each powerful stroke.

Upward, downward, upward, downward.

Until the music in his head beat strong and loud, taking him with it until his toes curled for the final time and he shuddered as wave after wave of liquid fire poured from his body and soul.

Almost immediately, Lianne joined him, her own body convulsing and the heat of her own release taking her over the edge. She collapsed on him, her lips finding his as she lowered herself onto him.

I'm in love with him!
I'm in love with Mason Sinclair!

Lianne wrapped her arms around the sleeping Mason and watched him with the amazement of her discovery.

She was in love!

And for some reason, the declaration was nothing to fear.

In the distance she heard a cell phone ring. Mason jumped up, noticing her there, but moved immediately to his phone.

He chatted for several minutes and then came back to her. "We have to leave," he said. "Alana is on the way to the hospital with Taurean. She's gone into labor. I want to be there for my brother."

"I'll get my stuff. I'm already packed. I won't be long. I left most of my things back at the resort."

She sprinted up the stairs and in a few minutes was back down.

* * *

When Mason arrived at the hospital, it took all his willpower not to rush up the flight of stairs to the floor where the delivery room was. But then he realized he knew nothing about the Queen Elizabeth Hospital and would have to wait for Bertha. The drive to the hospital had been a quiet but strange one. Bertha had driven her red car with a speed and skill that surprised him for a woman of her age. Of course, there were moments when he'd wanted to beg her to let him take a taxi, but he didn't want to offend the bubbly woman who talked nonstop.

When they'd finally reached the maternity ward, he quickly picked out Marc, Taurean's partner and close friend.

"Marc, how's she doing?"

"Taurean went into the delivery room with Alana, but we haven't heard anything yet. I'm sure everything will be all right."

"Come sit over here. Bertha, you come join us."

For the next few hours they sat, each in their own thoughts, each worried about Alana, but trusting God that she'd be all right.

The silence was broken by footsteps, and Taurean appeared. Mason leaped to his feet, followed by Marc and Bertha.

"Okay, no need to panic all. It's another girl. She's small, but strong and doing fine. She's just six and a half pounds, but the doctor says her lungs and heart are strong."

"Thank God," Bertha said. "And how's Alana?"

"A bit tired, but she's fine, too. I'm going to go back in to her. Mason can come with me and see her. I'll let him come back and let you know how beautiful my daughter is. For now, only family can come in. I'm going to stay with them overnight. Marc, can Melissa stay with you and Anne overnight?"

"Of course, Taurean. The girls will be delighted."

"Come, Mason."

Mason followed, internalizing the significance of what Taurean had said. Emotions he'd kept buried threatened to overwhelm him.

When they reached the ward, Taurean led him to the window. Four newborns dressed in pink lay in the tiny incubators. The baby closest to them opened her eyes and Mason knew immediately who she was. Bright brandy-colored eyes stared back at him.

"Isn't she beautiful?" his brother said.

Mason looked closely at the baby. He'd always wondered how people could call a newborn baby with wrinkly pale skin beautiful. But now he realized.

The new Buchanan baby was beautiful.

"Yes, and she has our eyes. She's definitely a Buchanan."

* * *

Mason watched as the red car pulled away. The trip back to the resort had been totally different. Bertha had kept him in stitches with her stories of Melissa and the two Blackman girls. They seemed truly a handful and always up to mischief.

When he entered the lobby, he called up to Lianne's room, hoping to invite her to dinner. It would be his last few days on the island, and he wasn't sure if he wanted to leave her yet, but knew she had to be back to the U.S. the next day. He was the one on official leave. He'd use those few days to think about his options. He'd definitely decided to stay in the Bureau, but he wasn't sure in what capacity.

There was no answer in her room, so he asked the receptionist if she'd seen Lianne, and was told that she'd left her key at reception and had said she was going to the beach.

When he reached the beach, he looked up and down, but despite the glow of the moonlight he couldn't see her. He glanced down, noticing the footprints headed in the direction of the rock where he liked to sit and chat with Beach. Maybe he shouldn't disturb her. She'd probably come out here to think, but he needed to talk to her.

He walked slowly, aware now that he did not carry his cane for most of the day. But he knew he should not overdo it. He should have brought it with him.

As he drew near to his favorite spot, he noticed her sitting there. She had her back to him, her head tilted upward as if she were in some intimate conversation with the moon. He heard her laughter and then silence again. The moon shone its white brilliance on her and she stretched her arms out as if trying to embrace its wonder and mystery.

Most people tried to catch a falling star, but Lianne was different. He knew she'd listened to what he'd said.

He wished he could paint like Alana. He'd paint Lianne just like this—her hair down, almost reaching the curve of her back, and the moon caressing her.

And then there was an unexpected bark and Beach appeared from behind the rock. He continued to bark and then realized that it was Mason. The tone of the barking changed and he raced toward Mason, excitement evident in the frantically wagging tail.

"So how's my boy today?"

Beach stopped right before him and sat, his head tilted, and looked up at Mason.

Mason reached down, touching his head gently. The dog fell to the ground, rolled over and exposed his tummy. Mason knew he wanted to be tickled.

He obliged.

"He missed you," Lianne said. He didn't realize she'd moved.

"Yes, it seems that way."

"You've been the only friend he's had in months. He recognized that. Wonder what he's going to do when you leave?"

"I never thought about that."

"You can take him with you. I'm sure if he has his shots it won't be a problem."

"I have a few more days on the island. I'll look into taking him with me. Come sit over here with me."

He led her back to where she'd been sitting.

"So where do we go from here, Lianne? Do we just call tonight the last time we see each other? I don't know if I could bear to leave you."

"I know what you mean. I've been here thinking about us. Damn, I've been stupid. I've known all along what has been happening. And just didn't want to admit that I was in love."

"In love?"

"Yes, Mason Sinclair, I'm hopelessly in love with you and I don't know what to do."

"I do."

"Do what?"

"Know what we can do."

"And what's that?"

"We can get married. If you'd do me the honor of accepting my proposal."

"You want to marry me?"

"Do I need to spell it out? Get on my knees, which isn't too possible with the state of my left leg? But yes, I want to marry you."

Silence.

"I just have to find one thing out before I give you a response."

"And what's that?"

"Not you. I have to ask Beach if he'll mind having me around."

Mason laughed, but went along with the silly game when Lianne turned to Beach, who was watching them as if they'd gone crazy. All he wanted to do was play, but he seemed to respect the fact that they were having an adult conversation.

When Lianne looked up, her eyes said it all. She placed her arms around Mason and said, "Yes, I'll marry you."

"Woman, I love you so much."

"I love you, too, Mason. When you came here, I was doing just what you told me. I was reaching for my dream, embracing the moonlight."

"Honey, we'll do that together. We'll make dreams of our own. It's easier to embrace the moonlight when you have someone to help."

And with that, Mason took her in his arms, the rays of the moon touching them with magic.

Chapter 14

The bells of the church ceased their ringing as the limousine drove away, carrying the newlyweds. On the church step stood the family and friends of Lianne and Mason Sinclair-Buchanan.

Taurean watched with pride the ever-growing members of his family. Ten years ago, he'd lost a brother and he'd paid dearly for his actions. But God had seen fit to send him happiness, and now his brother would have that same happiness.

His brother.

He'd lost one brother, but gained another. And Mason was his brother in every sense of the word.

It was not only a connection by blood, but during the past few months he'd grown to love his brother with as much passion as he did the other members of his family.

In his arms he held the latest addition to the family. Joanne Bertha Buchanan.

He hoped his daughter wouldn't hate him for that middle name but he'd promised Bertha Gooding that he'd give the baby her name.

In the distance, he saw Melissa, his other daughter. He loved this new baby, but Melissa would always be the child of his heart.

His brother Daniel was not here and he felt an overwhelming sadness at his younger brother's absence, but Daniel could not celebrate.

Two months ago, his wife and child had been killed in an accident and no one knew where he was. Daniel had just disappeared, leaving his church behind.

Though he was worried, Taurean knew his brother and knew that in time Daniel would return home. He needed time to grieve and heal.

The other new member to his family was Carolyn Sinclair, Mason's mother. Taurean was glad his mother had been willing to put the past behind and not only embrace Mason but accept Carolyn with genuine friendship.

Taurean looked up to the sky, acknowledging the presence of the Almighty.

* * *

Mason watched his wife as she came toward the bed, her naked body stirring him as it did each time he saw her.

"So how does it feel to be Mrs. Lianne Sinclair-Buchanan?"

"I'm not sure, Mr. Sinclair-Buchanan, but I intend to find out right now."

Mason smiled, feeling the familiar stirring of his manhood.

Yes, he wondered what his wife had in store for him tonight.

He loved surprises.

He glanced out the window, catching a brief glimpse of the moon.

Mason smiled.

Dreams did come true.

Leila Owens didn't know
how to love herself let alone
an abandoned baby
but Garret Grayson knew
how to love them both.

She's My Baby

Adrianne Byrd

(Kimani Romance #10)

AVAILABLE SEPTEMBER 2006
FROM KIMANI™ ROMANCE

Love's Ultimate Destination

Available at your favorite retail outlet.

Visit Kimani Romance at www.kimanipress.com.
KRABSMB

Single mom Haley Sanders's
heart was DOA.

Only the gorgeous
Dr. Pierce Masterson could
bring it back to life.

Sweet Surrender

Michelle Monkou

(Kimani Romance #11)

AVAILABLE SEPTEMBER 2006
FROM KIMANI™ ROMANCE

Love's Ultimate Destination

Available at your favorite retail outlet.

Visit Kimani Romance at www.kimanipress.com.

KRMMSS

He found *trouble* in paradise.

Mason Sinclair's visit to Barbados was supposed to be about uncovering family mysteries not the mysteries of Lianne Thomas's heart.

EMBRACING
THE MOONLIGHT
(Kimani Romance #12)

Wayne Jordan

AVAILABLE SEPTEMBER 2006

FROM KIMANI™ ROMANCE

Love's Ultimate Destination

Available at your favorite retail outlet.

Visit Kimani Romance at www.kimanipress.com.

KRWJETM

Silhouette® Desire®

Introducing an exciting appearance
by legendary
New York Times bestselling author

DIANA PALMER

HEARTBREAKER

He's the ultimate bachelor...
but he may have just met
the one woman to change his ways!

Join the drama in the story of a confirmed
bachelor, an amnesiac beauty and their
unexpected passionate romance.

"Diana Palmer is a mesmerizing storyteller
who captures the essence of what
a romance should be."—*Affaire de Coeur*

Heartbreaker *is available from Silhouette Desire
in September 2006.*

Visit Silhouette Books at www.eHarlequin.com   SDDPIBC

Introducing…

nocturne

a spine-tingling new line from Silhouette Books.

These paranormal romances will seduce you with dark, passionate tales that stretch the boundaries of conflict, desire, and life and death, weaving a tapestry of sensual thrills and chills!

Don't miss the first book...

UNFORGIVEN

by *USA TODAY* bestselling author

LINDSAY McKENNA

Launching October 2006, wherever books are sold.

SNIBC